9/18

WHY CAN'T
I BE YOU

Also by Melissa Walker

Let's Pretend We Never Met

WHY CAN'T I BE YOU

Melissa Walker

HARPER

An Imprint of HarperCollinsPublishers

Library of Congress Control Number: 2018933353
ISBN 978-0-06-256720-8

Typography by Alison Klapthor
18 19 20 21 22   CG/LSCH   10 9 8 7 6 5 4 3 2 1
❖
First Edition

For Cousin Curry, thank you
for all the summers that have been and will be

Chapter 1

When I reach underneath my bed to look for Ronan's Transformer, here is what I find:

Dust balls. People sometimes call them "bunnies," but that doesn't make sense to me. They're balls, or maybe floating masses. But bunnies? No.

A red plastic spear, which could be mistaken for a toothpick. I know, however, that it's the broken end of Darth Vader's lightsaber from my six-year-old birthday cake topper.

A puzzle piece with blue flowers on it.

That last thing makes me go *oh!*, because it's my mom's. She does puzzles and then glues them together and frames them. They're all over our walls. And this particular puzzle, with blue hydrangeas, has been missing its last piece for almost a year.

I stick it in my back pocket—Mom will be so happy.

"Can't find it!" I shout to Ronan as I head out the screen door and onto our tiny square of porch where he's waiting in the plastic lawn chair.

"Well, keep an eye out," he says with a scowl.

"What do you need it for anyway?" I ask him. We're eleven now, and I don't think he plays Transformers anymore. Does he?

"It's lucky," he mumbles.

"What?" I'm not sure I heard him right.

"I just want it back. Okay, Claire?" he says, his face softening a little as he closes his eyes to the bright June sunlight. Ronan's freckles are just starting to show on his pale skin as the summer sun gets more intense, and his sandy-brown hair is growing longer, shaggy. It looks good that way, like how boys on TV wear theirs.

I wonder if the Transformer search has anything to do with his father being back, but I don't ask.

"Anyway."

He says that word a lot lately with nothing to follow it. Like "anyway" means something. Still he stays, unmoving, in the chair on our porch square, so I think he wants to talk more.

I sit down on the top step to wait, since there's only the one chair and our porch isn't big enough for both of us, which is one of the reasons why "porch" is a generous word. I think you have to be able to fit two seats in an area for it to be called something as sociable as a porch.

I pick at the strings on the edges of my jean shorts as I wait for Ronan to talk, because he will . . . eventually. It's the start of summer break, and our moms are at work; he tends to talk when there is no one else around but me.

This is the first summer I'm allowed to stay home alone. Last year I went to a YMCA camp because Mom helps clean the gym on Saturdays, but it was a lot of craft-making and running drills, neither of which are my thing. I only really like the court time—basketball is my favorite sport. In a couple of years I'll be old enough to be a counselor-in-training, which Mom wants me to do, but I figured out a way to convince her to let me stay home this summer.

"I've heard that free time is really good for kids," I told Mom. And then I quoted a poster that was in my guidance counselor's office last year: "'How can I be curious if I don't have time to dream?'"

"My little girl is almost twelve." Mom had let out this low sigh, and then she looked at me with her mushy emotional face and I knew she was saying yes. This summer is my moment between going to kids' camp and having to do more grown-up working stuff. I turn twelve in August. So does Ronan. Our birthdays are three days apart, actually. And we live next door to each other in Twin Pines Trailer Park.

"Are you going to Brianna's party?" Ronan asks after a long silence.

"Yeah," I say. "Her new house has a pool, so it's a pool party! Jealous?"

"I'm going too," he says, sitting up and finally looking at me. "Mom left the invitation out for me this morning."

"Oh," I say. "I thought it was just girls." It's always

been just girls. A boy-girl pool party . . . why didn't Brianna say so?

Ronan stands up. "Well, I'll be there," he says, and then he starts to head back to his place.

"Where are you going now?" I ask him. Because I kind of thought the Transformer thing was an excuse to come over, to hang out with me for the day. I'm pretty bored, and Brianna is busy unpacking because they only just moved this week.

Ronan says, "Home." And that doesn't leave me much to work with.

I sit out on the porch and text Brianna. It takes forever to go through because Twin Pines is in a dead zone where the signal only works if the clouds are hanging just so in the sky, as my mom says. That's why we still have a regular phone too.

Claire: Your pool party is boy-girl?

Waiting. Watching. Wind blowing the long grass around Mrs. Gonzalez's trailer because she's older, and even though we have an every-now-and-then person who comes to mow, she's on the edge of the field and it grows really fast and wild there. I kind of like it wild though—she gets lots of those fluffy-seed dandelions you can blow in people's faces, and she doesn't mind if we pick them so Ronan and I can have Flower Wars. My bedroom window looks out on her yard, and I used to angle myself so I could only see her wild patches. I'd pretend I lived in the countryside, with tangled spots of flowers and long, arching grass.

Finally. A ding.

Brianna: yes! eden says it'll be better

Eden. That's Brianna's cousin who's visiting for the summer. I met her last year when she was in town for a few days. She's twelve, but a grade older, so almost thirteen.

I don't want to have a too-big reaction to the party news, so I just text back *cool*.

I kick off my dusty flip-flops and go inside, escaping the heat and thinking about maybe putting some tea bags into a pitcher for sun tea.

Mom will be happy when she gets back and finds her puzzle piece and a cold pitcher of sugary tea spread out like offerings on our folding table. She likes it when I'm "productive."

But first I go into my room and find the invitation that came in the mail yesterday. It's on the nightstand next to my bed, and I open it up carefully so I don't tear the shiny peach envelope. The paper inside is thick, almost like cardboard, and the writing is cursive and fancy.

You're invited to the twelfth birthday of
Miss Brianna Lane Foley
Saturday the 23rd of June
at 3 o'clock in the afternoon
415 Hobson Terrace
Bring your bathing suits!
Regrets only 555-4350

Now I'm starting to think Ronan came over just to brag about being invited! I wonder which other boys will be there.

And I wonder how often Brianna is talking to Eden, or when that started. I guess it makes sense to include boys now that we're going to be twelve. I don't have big birthday parties—it's usually just me, Mom, and Dad, but I realize that if friends were invited, those friends would include Ronan, so technically I'm a boy-girl party kind of person.

But still. A boy-girl pool party . . . why didn't Brianna tell me?

Chapter 2

Mom comes home late in the afternoon and I'm watching TV. "Clairebear!" Her voice is bright and I know it was a good day. "I brought you a new swimsuit!"

I stand up to give her a side hug. She smooths my hair as I lean into her soft T-shirt.

"Have a look," she says. "Tags and everything. The Skylers are going up to the lake through August, so Mrs. Skyler bought a bunch of suits. This one was a little too small for Gemma so . . . it's yours."

I pick up the two-piece suit with neon triangles on it. It's cute. Maybe not what I would choose, but definitely wearable. When I glance at the price tag, I know it must be a good brand even though I don't recognize the name. Gemma Skyler wouldn't get anything less. She's two years older than I am, and Mom's been cleaning the Skylers' house since we were kids. When we were really little Gemma and I would play together while Mom worked. Her tree house is bigger than my bedroom—we had a lot of fun there.

"Thanks, Mom," I say. Now I have a new bathing suit to wear to Brianna's party.

"You're welcome, baby."

"Oh! I have something for you too," I tell her, moving aside so she can see my welcoming table setup. "I made sun tea, and look what I found . . ." I pick up the blue-flowered puzzle piece and wave it in front of her eyes.

"The missing piece!" She grabs it and hurries over to the tray by the TV where she's kept the hydrangea puzzle, unfinished, for months. Mom fits the last piece in, and I see her body actually relax. She likes completion. She doesn't even blame me for losing the piece, and I'm glad.

"Where will you put this one?" I ask her. The walls in our hallway are already filled with framed puzzles.

"I'm thinking in the kitchen," she says. "When we look at it, it'll be like we have fresh flowers on the counter each day." Then she yawns, even though it's only four thirty in the afternoon. "Okay, Clairebear, I'm gonna take a shower."

While the water runs, I pour a glass of ice tea and sit on the couch with the catalog Mom brought in from the mailbox. Then there's a knock on our screen door.

It's Ronan. He's changed into a nice shirt.

"Hey," he says. "I need your help."

Ten minutes later, Ronan and I are standing at the top of the hill in Cleland Cemetery, which is the closest place nearby where my phone can get a solid signal. Ronan has an old flip phone that doesn't go online, so I'm his internet source when he can't use his family computer.

At first his face looked so serious that I got worried, but it turned out that he just wanted a good phone camera to take a picture of himself. So I yelled to Mom that I'd be back soon, and I walked out with him.

"What do you need this for, anyway?" I ask him. Then I get a suspicion. "Are you allowed to be on social media?" I'm not until I'm thirteen. Mom says that's when it's legal.

"Just take the picture, Claire," he says in response, so I snap him wearing his new-looking striped polo shirt and standing in front of the big old oak tree that makes a nice backdrop, as long as I don't get any of the gravestones in the bottom of the frame.

I glance at the image on my screen. Ronan looks older, like a teenager already, in his nice shirt. I notice that his jaw seems more grown-up, if a jaw can be such a thing. It's sharp angled and tough looking.

Ronan grabs the phone from me.

"That'll work." He forwards it to his email, and his face goes from serious to smiling when he says, "Wanna hit the brook?"

I nod. I've been waiting to get to the brook all day. It's nearly ninety-five degrees out.

Ronan starts running, and I'm on his heels; I've always been *almost* as fast as he is. He kicks off his fake

Crocs at the edge of the water, but I barrel on in with my flip-flops. "They're water shoes!" I say when he looks at me funny. "And so are yours."

He laughs. "I forgot!" he says, climbing into the green rubber shoes and then wading back out to me. There are tiny pebbles under the water, so shoes help.

We make our way to the big black rock just around the southern bend of the brook from the clearing where we entered. I think of it as our rock, mine and Ronan's, though I've never said that out loud.

I scramble up and settle myself on the butt-size ledge at the top while Ronan leans against the broad side of the rock and closes his eyes. There's something sad about the way he does it slowly, for the second time today, like he can't handle the daylight anymore.

"You should bring Ellie here with us sometime," I say. Ellie is Ronan's pet lizard. He got her when his dad left, I guess because his mom felt bad or something. I don't think a lizard replaces a dad, but Mom told me it isn't for me to say.

Ronan grins. He loves Ellie. He named her after our student teacher that year, Miss Ellie, who always let

Ronan sit by her side at morning meeting that spring when his dad went away.

"I taught her to flick out her tongue on command," he says.

"No way!"

"Yup. All I have to do is stick out my tongue and she does it back."

"Cool. I think Ellie is an uncharacteristically smart lizard."

"I like it when you use eight-syllable words," Ronan says.

Then we count *uncharacteristically* out on our hands, and he's right. Eight syllables.

We're quiet for a while, me sitting up high and Ronan standing, leaning with our rock against his back. Even though it feels still and humid where we are, there's a little breeze up high. It's working its way through the green leaves above me, making them twitch and dance.

"You know why I love this place?" Ronan asks.

"Why?"

"Because there's no them, there's just us," he says. And I know he's talking about his parents—his dad, really. Mr. Michaels left their family for, like, two years, and now he's back. It must be weird.

I love this place too for that reason, and others. Even in the winter I like to come down here and crack the ice that forms around the edge of the water—it breaks into pretty patterns that look like magic. But the summer, right now, is the brook's best time.

Usually it's just Ronan and me here. There aren't any other kids our age at Twin Pines Trailer Park—it's mostly older people with what my mom calls "fixed incomes" and people who move in for a few months and move out again. I really don't get to know everyone who comes and goes in the park, but the ones who've been my neighbors all along, like Mrs. Gonzalez and Ronan and his mom, they feel like family.

I turn my eyes down and notice that Ronan's hair is getting lighter from the sun already. It looks like all the colors on a box of Honey Nut Cheerios that goes from a darker brown to a brighter blond. I love naming colors, and I'd call Ronan's hair *Harvest Gold*.

A fish jumps in the deep area, and Ronan looks up at me quickly with wide eyes like, *Did you see?*

"Your hair looks like a cereal box," I say, and he gives me a shrug. He's used to me saying weird stuff.

"Shoulda brought my rod," he says.

"Hey, did you know Gemma Skyler gets to spend the whole summer at the lake?" I ask. I know Ronan always wishes he could get to Town Lake, which everyone calls "the lake," to fish. But it's, like, an hour away and his mom works a lot. Maybe his dad will take him this summer.

Ronan raises his eyebrow and says, "Anyway." He starts hunting for flat rocks to skip, and then he throws a few across the brook's surface with an expert wrist-snap. The last one skips about ten times, and I let out a loud whistle.

"Who's the king?" asks Ronan, and I like seeing his smile big and bold like this, going all the way to his eyes.

From up on the rock I give him a deep, seated bow. "Your Majesty."

He laughs, and then his head turns toward Twin Pines. "Did you hear that?"

"What?"

"Rocky," he says. "We'd better get home."

Rocky is the dog that lives behind Ronan with Mr. Brewster, a new neighbor who moved in last winter. It seems like Mr. Brewster might stay in our neighborhood, at least for a while, because he built a little pen next to his trailer for Rocky. Mr. Brewster works a lot and he told Ronan he wants Rocky to be able to be outside. The dog is a big, sweet goofball, a rescue bulldog mix, and Ronan is crazy about him. Mr. Brewster gave Ronan an extra leash when he saw their bond, so Ronan takes Rocky for walks sometimes. And the thing is, for some reason Rocky *really* doesn't like Ronan's dad. He's been barking a ton since Mr. Michaels came back.

Ronan reaches up to help me down from the rock, but I push off and jump into the brook, kicking up a pretty good splash in the shallow water—and his shorts get wet.

"Jerk," he says, but I hear the smile underneath. We walk close to each other as the sky gets dusky on the way home.

When we reach our trailers I start to wave goodbye, but he says, "Wanna come in?" and I have the feeling he needs me to, so I say yes.

Ronan's dad is on the couch watching TV. When he sees me, he doesn't get up or even move. His hair is long and his face is stubbly, but that's how I remember him from before too, maybe with fewer gray patches.

"Claire Ladd," he says, drawing out my full name like it's ten syllables instead of two. His voice sounds far away, like he's on the other side of a long tunnel even though he's right in front of me.

"Hi, Mr. Michaels," I say.

He doesn't say anything else, just turns back to the TV.

I glance over at Ronan, but he's looking down. The space feels dark somehow, like even though the TV is blasting and the corner lamp is on and there are three of us in this room, there's an emptiness here too.

"We wanted to ask if Ronan could come over to my house for dinner," I say before I can think. I look over at Ronan, and he lifts up his head.

Mr. Michaels nods slowly.

"Great," I say, and I take Ronan's hand. "I'll see you around, Mr. Michaels."

He doesn't respond.

When we get outside, Ronan squeezes my hand before he drops it, but he doesn't say a word. Best friends don't have to talk about things that feel bad.

Chapter 3

The dressing room at Belding's Department Store echoes when we laugh. That's one of the best parts of trying on clothes here.

"Wait till you see this next one," says Brianna. "I have two words: orange ruffles."

I giggle in anticipation.

The mall is empty today, and the salespeople don't seem to mind me and Brianna bringing six fancy dresses at a time from the juniors' section and pulling them on and off while we trade back and forth. We're the only ones here, so we come out into the middle area with the three-way mirrors and show each other what we're wearing with spins and silly dances.

There are some truly ugly formal dresses out there, and that's what Brianna and I go for first—the oddest colors and fabrics and shapes to make us look like rainbow cartoon characters.

I'm really into colors, and as soon as I learned to read I memorized all the names in Mom's makeup kit—they have better names than crayons. Who would choose boring old beige over *Ocean Sands* or *Metallic Mocha*, two sparkly browns I've seen in her eye shadow palette? Brianna says there are people whose job it is to figure out what to call makeup colors. Now that's a dream. I practice by trying to name our dress shades as we try them on. *Teal for Real* for a blue so bright it made my eyes hurt, *Scarlett Fever* for a deep-red one, and *Cream Dream* for a mostly white dress with weird gold swirls.

When we have on our fourth dresses—me in teal ruffles and Brianna in scarlet sequins—we flop down on the love seat next to the mirrors for a break.

"Oh! I forgot to tell you . . . Guess who's my new neighbor?" Brianna is smiling like it's going to be someone amazing. But there aren't any famous people in our town. That I know of.

"Who?" I ask.

"Emily Wu!"

"Oh," I say. Is that all? Emily Wu is a girl in our grade. She's popular, I guess you could say.

Brianna stands up and does a happy spin with her arms in the air. *Is she really excited about Emily Wu?* Then she bumps my arm. "You don't remember ballet class?" she asks.

I smile. I forgot. We all took ballet classes at the YMCA when we were, like, three.

"The spins!" Brianna and I laugh-shout at the same time.

Emily used to sit on the sidelines in ballet because she always said she had "the spins." And when our teacher forced her to dance she'd spin and spin, like she was one of those toy tops.

"You better watch out or she'll spin over to your house and knock over all your stuff," I say.

I stand up too, and we both start pirouetting around the room in our poufy dresses, our bright skirts flying out from our legs in streams of color, until we fall into the soft chairs, giggling loudly.

"I'm pretty sure she can walk straight these days," says Brianna.

"Well, just tell her to be careful around your pool."

We grin at each other.

"Hey, let's do something different now," Brianna says.

"Like what?" I ask.

"Let's try to find actual pretty dresses for each other."

"Why?" That doesn't sound like much fun.

"Just to see," says Brianna.

I'm about to ask, "To see what?" but she's already rushing out of the dressing room and back to the racks.

I hang up the blue pouf I tried on—it looks more like an ice-skating costume than a party dress. I always make sure to put back the clothes neatly and in the same place where I got them. I grab a couple of things from Brianna's dressing room to return too—she's a little messier than I am.

And then I think, *What the heck?* And I look

through the racks in a new way, actually trying to find something pretty. It makes me feel both excited and nervous, like I'm pretending to be older.

There's a whole row of black dresses that are more plain, and I usually pass right by that section when we're after showy looks, but now I slow down and move the hangers around so I can see the shape of each one. Brianna is shorter than I am, with pale skin and dark-brown hair. She always looks pretty in strappy dresses, so I find one for her with a simple top and a full skirt.

When I get into the dressing room, she's holding out a light-blue gown for me. It has two layers, a silky one underneath and a soft see-through one on top. The skirt is swishy and pleated, and the top is fitted.

"That's not going to look good," I say.

"I think it will," she says.

"Here." I hand her the black dress, and she raises her eyebrows skeptically.

"We're trusting each other, right?"

She nods, and we go into our own curtained rooms.

Before I even get my dress fully zipped in the back, I can tell Brianna was right. It's pretty. The color makes my skin look glowing instead of pale, and my brown eyes pick up the lightness of the blue somehow—they shine. Even my hair, which I always think of more in terms of what color it's not (not brown, not blond, but somewhere in between), seems to take on a richer tone that I'd call *Cinnamon*. The skirt swishes down to just above my knees and the middle part makes it look like I have a waist. My arms even look good because of the sleeve style—it can be worn on top of my shoulders or off the sides, which Mom wouldn't allow.

But that doesn't matter because this is all imaginary anyway, so when I walk out, I pull the sleeves down and it's officially off-the-shoulder.

Brianna comes out at the same time, and her dress, with thin spaghetti straps and a tulip-shaped skirt that's long and a little bit flared, fits her just like I thought it would. She looks mysterious and magical in that dress, like Snow White with a personality.

When I see myself in the triple mirror, I feel like I'm looking at an older me, one with more . . . everything. It's not that it makes my body look curvier, though it does. And it's not that the light-blue color of the dress looks like something a princess or a movie star would wear, but that's true too. It's that I look like me, but not. Like future me, or a person I could be if I were just a little bit different.

We stand together in front of the triple mirror and look at ourselves and then each other. We're both quiet at first, until we start talking at the same time.

"You look amazing!" says Brianna.

"That dress is perfect!" I say.

We laugh and look back at the mirror, both flushed with feeling pretty at the same time.

"There's a seventh-grade dance in the spring," says Brianna.

I nod and try to see the tag under my arm. I haven't looked at the price of anything because we always try on dresses and it's just a joke, but when I get a glimpse and read eighty-eight dollars, I realize that I couldn't ever have this blue dress. I feel my heart thump an ouch.

"Let's take a picture," I say, trying to sound upbeat.

"Good idea!" Brianna runs back into her dressing room for her phone, and we both pose a few different ways and then we take solo pics.

"I seriously might ask my mom for this dress," she says to me.

And I smile and nod again, before I head into the dressing room to take mine off. I don't look in the mirror as I leave it hanging alone in the tiny curtained room. I shake off the thought of how the dress looked on me, making me feel like someone else for a minute.

We head to the food court to get lunch, and we both order combo meals.

"What do you think seventh grade is going to be like?" asks Brianna as we slurp our Cokes. We both think it tastes better with sound, even though our moms say it's rude.

"I don't know," I say, and in my head I'm thinking about how I liked having my shoulders bare and I wish that someone from school, besides Brianna, had seen me in that *Bora-Bora* blue dress, by accident or something.

"Eden says everything changes in seventh grade," says Brianna.

Eden again. "Like what?" I ask.

"Like *everything*."

"That's dumb," I say.

Brianna laughs and bumps my arm softly. "Don't say that about my cousin."

"I didn't say Eden was dumb, I said her idea was." I drink the last of my soda with a big straw-slurp finish. "What does that even mean, *everything changes?*"

Brianna shrugs. "She's coming tomorrow," she says, "so you can ask her yourself."

Chapter 4

My dad calls Friday "Claireday" because it's our once-a-week date. He lives in an apartment complex that's half an hour away, but every Friday, right at 5:45 p.m., he comes over to pick me up and take me out. Sometimes I sleep at his place for the weekend, it's part of the custody agreement, but not tonight. Often Dad has to work long days on Saturdays, and I like my room better at Mom's, so we're all flexible.

"Have fun!" Mom calls out the door as we pull away in Dad's old El Camino. It's bright blue, a color I call *Aqua Dream*, and it's got the front of a car and the back of a truck, which sort of reminds me of one of those dogs with big heads and small bodies, but in reverse. He loves this car, and he calls it Charlie. Tonight it's warm and the windows are rolled all the way down.

Dad beeps Charlie's horn in response to Mom. They're friendly, my parents, but they don't do anything together unless it's for me, like a birthday or holiday or something. They were married for two years after I was born, but they were pretty young then and they say they "grew apart." They both use those exact words, so I guess they agree on it. I don't remember us ever living all together, and we've had Claireday since I was in preschool, so even though sometimes someone will hear my parents are divorced and then look at me with an "oh that must be hard" face, I don't really feel like it is.

"Where to, Clairebear?" asks Dad, working the toothpick that's always in the side of his mouth. He's wearing his cool-guy sunglasses and a baseball cap that says "Bass Master." He looks like he hasn't shaved in a while, but that works for him. He's handsome, especially when he showers off the dirt from his construction jobs—he's a contractor, so he's mostly in charge now and not doing the labor, but he still sweats a lot. When I don't answer, he says, "It's a beautiful night. Corn dogs and mini golf?"

"Sure." I press in the big button that turns Dad's old-timey radio tuner to my station—K101 Hits.

Dad puts his hands over his ears and mouths a silent scream, even though he programmed that station especially for me.

"Stop," I tell him with a laugh.

He grins at me and says, "Okay, a few songs. But then I'm putting on Bruce!"

My dad loves Bruce Springsteen. Like, a lot.

"Can I just have K101 for the ride there?" I ask. "Bruce is better for the ride home."

"Energy wise?" asks Dad.

I nod.

"Okay, I hear you," he says. And then he bobs his head crazy fast to a new single, and when we stop at a red light the lady in the car next to us laughs at him. Her window's down and everything, so we hear her.

"You're so embarrassed," I say to Dad.

"Never!" he says, raising his hand in a wave and

headbanging harder, even though this is a hip-hop song and that's not really the right move.

The lady laughs again, and so do I.

When we pull away from the light the lady waves to us. I think we made her night better.

Dad's phone rings from the center of the seat, and he and I both look down at it. *K calling. . . .*

"Who's K?" I ask.

"Someone from work," Dad says as he silences the ring. But he said it really quickly. I open my mouth to ask more about "K," but Dad rushes in. "Hey, how was your week? First days of summer, huh?"

"Yeah." I shrug as I think about how even though summer has barely started, things have felt kind of weird. But I don't know how to talk about that, so I just say, "I found a missing puzzle piece for Mom."

Dad laughs. "I'm sure that made her truly happy." He says it sincerely, like he's appreciating the way Mom is. "So what, besides playing puzzle detective, have you been up to this week?"

"Nothing really," I say. "The brook, the mall, the seventh-grade reading list . . . oh, and Brianna moved!

Her new pool will be ready to swim in soon!"

"Well now, that's cool," says Dad.

"Yeah, she's having a pool party for her birthday, and even Ronan is invited," I tell him.

"They're friends, aren't they, Brianna and Ronan?"

Dad tries to keep up with things, and he does pretty well, but he doesn't get some parts, like how when you're eleven girls and boys aren't *friends* anymore. Ronan and I are sort of an exception. And even with us we're more at-home friends than anything because when people are around, my being close to him means they say "ooh." It doesn't bother me, but I've seen his face get red.

"Yeah, they're friends," I say. It's easier not to get into these details.

We pull up to Minnie's Golf, and Dad leans out of Charlie's window. He whistles loudly. "Melinda!" he yells to Minnie, the owner. He knows her from high school.

Up at the counter, Minnie gives us a big wave. Her bright-pink lips are pressed into a heart-shaped smile.

"Hi, Rick, Claire," says Minnie. "Date night?"

"Claireday," says my dad. "And we just couldn't stay

away from your lovely establishment."

"Right." Minnie smirks at him, but I can tell she's glad to see us.

Dad winks at me before he comes around to open my door. It's a thing he does, and I see Minnie smile at his gentlemanly move. People like my dad. They find him charming, but it's not the fake sort of charming. He's kind too. Like, deep down. People see that.

We go up to the window, and Dad pays for a round of mini golf. Then Minnie comes out from behind the half door at the counter to hand us our clubs.

"You're pregnant!" I say.

Minnie laughs. "I am," she says. "I'm about to turn thirty, so Joe and I figured it was time."

Dad leans over to me and whispers, "That's the right way to do it. When you're thirty!"

He says stuff like that a lot, about how he and Mom were too young to have a baby—me. It used to bother me, and one day when I was seven I told him so. Dad said, "Claire, I wouldn't trade you for a palace full of money or a world filled with Funyuns. You are my bear, and I love you as deep as the woods go. So maybe I say things like that, but it's not about you. I'm just talking about my foolish self."

Then he hugged me and I felt better. My dad really loves Funyuns.

Dad lets me take an extra shot on the second hole when my ball falls into the moat, and I let him have a do-over when the windmill blocks his ball and sends it right back to the starting green. We've been laughing and having a good time, but on the sixth hole, when Dad asks how Ronan is doing with his father being home, I feel funny and I wonder if he's been waiting to ask this question all night. I pretend to focus on lining up my ball, and I don't say anything for a minute. But Dad knows that, with me, quiet means there are words to dig for.

"Claire?" he pushes.

"Ronan's okay," I say. And then I decide to put the quiet on him. "He doesn't talk much about it. Or anything. You know how he is."

"I guess I do," he says. "Or at least I know how twelve-year-old boys are."

"We're not twelve yet," I say to Dad as I take one

final second to line up my shot.

"August is coming fast," says Dad, and then he does this low sigh just like Mom did the other day.

Seriously? Why does everyone act like turning twelve is a zombie apocalypse? Is there something I don't know? Like I'm going to turn into a raging monster maniac werewolf? *Gah!*

I get so worked up that I miss my shot.

Chapter 5

Early the next morning, Rocky starts barking and the noise wakes me up. I hear Ronan's mom's car pull out, and I yawn and run a hand through my hair, which I can tell is messy and all over the place. It's stringy and thin, and I wear it up so much that Mom says I should cut it, but I like the options of longer hair even if I don't use them. I grab the ponytail holder on the crate next to my bed.

After a stretch and a roll over to the other side for a minute, I'm fully awake. I have a plan today: ice cream.

When I get to the kitchen I decide to make breakfast for Mom as a surprise, so I get out butter, sugar, and cinnamon and put two pieces of bread in the toaster.

The microwave clock reads 7:14 a.m. when Rocky starts to bark again. He's been doing that a lot this morning, and I wonder if Mr. Michaels is outside. I haven't seen him leave their trailer at all. I peek out the kitchen window, and I see Ronan's dad walking around the raised plot next to their front porch. He's in a bathrobe and he's kind of shuffling, like someone in a zombie movie. A zombie, I guess. I close the half curtain so I can't see him anymore.

By the time the toaster pops up, the barking has quieted. I arrange the toast on two plates, the fancy china ones we got at the thrift shop last summer. They have a cherry blossom pattern, and I like to imagine that a royal family used them once. We got four of the plates but one broke last fall when I accidentally dropped it carrying dishes to the sink.

These two look pretty though, and when I put the toast on them I immediately pat each piece with butter so it'll melt a little before I try to spread it. That's key.

I shake the cinnamon and sugar into a small bowl, and once the butter is warmed and spread, I pinch the cinnamon sugar between two fingers and carefully sprinkle the mixture over the toast. The butter makes it stick.

I place the plates on top of our small round table and go to find the white cloth napkins Mom keeps in a drawer under the potholders. I know it'll add to the laundry load, which is one of my jobs around here, but I'm already using the china plates and it seems right to add nice napkins too.

Next to Mom's plate I put the envelope Dad gave me last night—the child support money for the month. Sometimes I wish he'd just mail it. Or that he'd hand it to her himself.

Mom comes out in a T-shirt and boxer shorts while I'm filling up small glasses of water.

"Well isn't this nice," she says, moving the envelope to her purse. I put down the glasses and pull out her chair for her. "What's the occasion?"

I shrug. "I felt like being fancy this morning."

Mom bites into her cinnamon toast. "Mmm . . . delicious," she says.

I sit up on my chair and join her. It *is* good.

"How's Dad?" asks Mom. She always politely asks this question, even though if she wanted to she could talk to him herself. It annoys me how they don't communicate directly. They're pleasant to each other, but it's like they own a business together, and that business is me.

"Fine," I say. "The same."

After mini golf, Dad and I got corn dogs and sat at one of the wooden picnic tables near the ninth hole. We talked about lots of things, but not about "K," which was what was on my mind, or about Ronan's dad, which it seemed like was on my dad's.

Mom yawns and stretches her arms. "I'm glad you guys had fun," she says, and even though I didn't tell her that specifically, she knows she can trust it—Dad and I always have fun together.

"Hey, Mom?" I start, and then I'm not sure what I want to ask exactly, but I'm still thinking about Mr. Michaels in his bathrobe, shuffling.

"Hmm?" She's licking the cinnamon from her fingers.

"Is Mr. Michaels . . . um . . . okay?"

She tilts her head, which is how I can tell she's going to answer carefully.

"He's not quite himself," she says, wiping her fingers on a napkin. "He struggles with depression, and he's trying to get better now, but it's not easy."

"Oh." I look down at my pretty plate and I wonder if Mr. Michaels is on medication or something, if that's why he looks so lost sometimes.

"He needs time," Mom says. "Why, did Ronan say something?"

I shake my head. "No, I was just wondering."

"As long as you're wondering and not worrying," she says. Then she claps her hands together. "So what's your Saturday plan?"

Mom has Sundays off, but she still works on Saturdays cleaning at the YMCA. "Ice cream," I tell her.

"Bus?" she asks.

I nod my head. The bus stops pretty close to the entrance to Twin Pines, and it's free in my town. Some kind of incentive to get people out of their cars. It goes right to Canefield Plaza, which isn't that great, it's just a strip of stores, but there's a Frosty's Ice Cream at one end.

"With Ronan?"

Even though the bus is safe and everything, Mom likes me to have a "buddy." I asked her not to use that word anymore when she's talking about me bringing a friend somewhere because it sounds so kindergarten, and she's been good about it. I nod again.

"Great idea," she says. Then she leans over to the couch next to the table and gets out her wallet. She hands me a ten-dollar bill. "For both of you," she says. "Tell Ronan it's my treat, okay?" And then I hear her whisper "Christina has enough to worry about" under her breath.

Mom is friends with Ronan's mom, Christina, who's a health aide for older people. Christina works weird hours, which is probably why she drove off at six thirty. Sometimes in the evenings she and Mom sit in chairs together in the yard between our trailers and drink beers with pieces of lime in them. But they haven't done that since Ronan's dad has been home.

After Mom leaves for the YMCA, I walk outside and feel that there's a little breeze. I go back in and pull on the army jacket Mom found at the thrift shop for me this spring—it's the best shade of faded green and we added some patches on the arm. It always makes me feel cool, and I roll up the sleeves as I walk over to Ronan's door. But then I remember Mr. Michaels and the shuffling. I pause, deciding to head around the back to where Ronan's window is. I knock lightly on the rectangular glass, but he doesn't peek out. Sometimes he sleeps in, and lately he seems more tired. I'll wait.

I go up the hill a little way until I get a strong signal so I can text Brianna to meet us at Frosty's. When I walk back down, I see Mrs. Gonzalez out in her raised vegetable bed—each trailer has one, but hardly anyone plants in them—checking on the tomatoes. She wears her hair in a black-gray bun high on her head. I've never seen it down, but the bun is really big, so I think it's crazy long. She has on a loose dress with big flowers on it like she always wears, and bright-blue Crocs. Those are new.

"Not yet?" I ask about the tomatoes. I can see they're still mostly green.

She shakes her head.

"Must be hard to wait," I say.

"It's okay," says Mrs. Gonzalez. "Change comes quickly. Sometimes overnight." She gives me a wink and a little smile as she walks back up the steps and into her trailer.

Chapter 6

look at my phone. It's after ten a.m. Ronan must be awake by now.

His front door is open, but the screen is shut, so I knock on that and it makes a rattling noise.

"Hello?" I call out as I step into Ronan's empty living room. The TV is on, the volume low, and there's a dark spot on the couch, a deep indentation. It smells stale in here, kind of gross. I immediately want to leave, but then I hear the rumbling.

Mr. Michaels is somewhere down the hall, talking in a low voice. I start to step backward, out of the living room, through the door and onto the porch again, but before I make it, a door slams and Mr. Michaels comes into the living room, bleary-eyed and bathrobed. He leans on the wall.

He sees me standing in the doorway, he must, but he lurches toward the couch and sits in the dark spot, turning his eyes to the TV like I'm not even here.

I have no idea what to say or do, so I stand there and stare at the picture of the beach that's above the couch. There are two seagulls near the top of the frame that look like they're holding hands. Or wings. Or whatever.

Finally, I call out, "Ronan?" and I've never been so happy to see my friend's freckled face as he emerges from the hallway and takes my hand to pull me out the door.

We haven't held hands this much since we were learning to cross the street.

"What's wrong?" I whisper to him as we walk farther and farther from his trailer.

He drops my hand.

"C'mon!" he says, and he takes off running. I can hear the bus coming up the street.

I race to catch him, and we wave frantically to get

the bus driver's attention. It works and she waits for us, smiling with all her teeth as we get on. Ronan pushes past her with a frown, but I say good morning and give her a shrug to apologize for him. Mom says that it's important to treat everyone nicely, and I've found that to be true.

I follow Ronan to the back of the bus, where he sits in the very last row and turns toward the window with his arms folded over himself.

He doesn't even know that I have this grand ice cream plan, he just wanted to get on the bus.

"You okay?" I ask.

Ronan's frown doesn't budge.

I bump against his shoulder. "I've got money for ice cream . . ." I pull out the ten-dollar bill my mom gave me. "Mom's treat."

Ronan's mouth turns up a tiny bit and that's enough for me. The sun streams through the big bus window onto our laps, and it feels warm but not too hot yet. The bus picks up a few more people, so there's a quiet buzz of "hello" every couple of minutes as I make a point to smile at everyone.

Soon Ronan's mood seems to warm up too, and by the time we get to our stop at Canefield Plaza he's in the middle of telling me about this movie he saw where all these kids in a small town fought a monster no one could see.

"At the end there was this huge explosion and they found out the monster wasn't even that big," he says. Then he yells "Have a good day!" to the bus driver as we get off in the back like you're supposed to.

At Frosty's, I order Chocolate Chunk in a cup and Ronan gets Vanilla Peanut Butter Swirl in a pretzel cone. I'm paying when I hear a shout from the door.

"Claire!"

Brianna walks into Frosty's with her hair down, which is weird because she's always wearing a ponytail. It looks nice, though, all shiny and fanned out over her shoulders. But even while I'm noticing Brianna, I can't help but be distracted by the girl behind her.

She's really tall, with the longest legs I've seen outside of a magazine. She has curly black hair that rises above her head like a cloud. She's wearing a jean jacket with the sleeves cut off and round, jet-black sunglasses.

Her lipstick is frosted pink. I'm staring at the girl's mouth, wondering what the color's called, when she blows a big blue bubble and pops it perfectly, without getting any gum on her face.

"Hey," the girl says in my direction. Wait, is she *with* Brianna?

Her voice is breathy and I can't tell if she's talking to me or Ronan, so I glance over at him. His mouth is wide open, and he looks like he's frozen in ice.

"You guys remember my cousin Eden," says Brianna.

Ho-ly sneakers.

I do, of course, remember Eden. The Eden of my memory has short black hair cropped close to her head, glasses, and bird-skinny legs. I've never met Brianna's aunt and uncle, but I know Eden's dad is black and her mom is white, so she has this smooth tan skin dotted with freckles, which is about the only thing that Old Eden and New Eden have in common. I suck in a breath.

New Eden walks up to the counter and leans over the edge. "Do you give tastes?" she asks the ice cream guy.

"Sure," he says, and his face looks just like Ronan's—

gobsmacked. Does my face look like that? Does Cousin Eden make every face look like that with her jean jacket and her frosted lips and her blue bubble gum?

Is this the same Eden from last summer? Is she really only twelve?

When she takes the wooden tester spoon I see that her nails are a flat white color, like she painted them with wall paint or something. Cool.

I feel a wet drop on my arm and look over to see Ronan's ice-cream cone tilted at an angle and dripping down onto me.

"Get a napkin!" I snap, and he finally unfreezes and clumsily tries to wipe us both. "Ugh, let's find a booth."

"We'll come sit with you guys," says Brianna, and Eden smiles as she raises her sunglasses to reveal the biggest brown eyes I've ever seen, with thin, jet-black, cat-eye liner that curves expertly past her lashes.

Whoa.

Chapter 7

Eden hasn't stopped talking since she sat down. Last year, she lived in a small town in Tennessee. Apparently, this year her mom sold a song to a country singer, so her whole family moved to Nashville.

"I go to the Bluebird all the time to hear music, and you should *see* who walks in . . . Kacey, Brad. And one night even *Maren*, you guys!"

I don't really know country music singers, but I get that last part. This girl hangs out with Maren Morris. Kind of.

"Gah!" I say, because she has a song that I really love

and that's the noise that comes out when I don't know what to say. "That's cool."

"Yeah," says Eden, looking pleased with my reaction. She takes a sip of her strawberry milkshake through a red-striped straw. Brianna got strawberry too, even though I know she likes vanilla best.

Brianna and I are on the inside of the booth across from each other, and Ronan and Eden are on the outside. I'm trying to catch Brianna's eye and give her a "what the heck, your cousin is a total goddess now" look, but Brianna is busy staring up at Eden adoringly. And I do mean *up*. Eden must be half a foot taller than the rest of us. Even Ronan.

Suddenly the whole boy-girl swim party suggestion coming from Eden makes sense. I'm wishing I could see a series of pictures or a movie montage of how she went from a glasses-wearing, short-haired smarty-pants to rock-star cool girl in less than one year.

Ronan is like a mannequin next to me. Well, a mannequin eating ice cream, because he has to finish his cone before it drips more. I bet he's glad for the activity so he doesn't have to keep up conversation with Eden, but as we sit there his eyes keep darting toward her and then away again.

"Ronan, I saw your new profile," says Brianna. "I followed you."

I tilt my head back and turn my eyes to Ronan. So that *is* what that photo was for.

He's smiling at Brianna and definitely not acknowledging my eyeballing as he says, "Cool."

"I'm Nash Queen with an underscore in the middle," says Eden, and I fight the urge to write it down. *Nash_Queen, Nash_Queen, Nash_Queen,* I repeat in my head. "I post pics of life in Nashville, mostly, and some selfies."

"I wish you could have a profile, Claire," says Brianna. "It's so much fun to keep up with people over the summer."

"Wait, you're not on social?" Eden looks at me.

I shake my head. "My mom won't let me until next year."

"How would she even know?" asks Eden. "You have a phone, right?"

"She'd know," I say. And I want to move on because I don't like the curl of Eden's pink upper lip. "Hey, is that a new ring?" I ask Brianna. I've been noticing that the pink stone matches the strawberry milkshake inching up her straw.

"Yeah," she says, spinning it on her finger. "Early birthday present."

"It's pretty," I say.

"Pink pearl," Eden chimes in. And at the same time we both say, "Brianna's birthstone."

Then Eden and I smile at each other, but my smile isn't real and I don't think hers looks very solid either.

"Are you excited about the pool party?" I ask Brianna.

But it's her cousin who responds. "Brianna's dad is letting us decorate the whole backyard like Hawaii, with tiki torches and floating flowers and everything," says Eden. "It's going to be *amaze*." She draws out *amaze* into *amaaaaaaze*. Why shorten a word if you're gonna do that?

"I can't wait to swim," I say, mostly to Brianna. "My

mom got me a new bathing suit. Well, it was Gemma Skyler's, but she never wore it, so now it's mine." Brianna knows some of my favorite clothes come from Gemma.

"That's awesome," says Brianna.

I nod, and I can feel Eden looking at me, so I stare back at her. She purses her rosy lips. I'd call that color *Pink Peeve*. "Speaking of . . . Bri, we should go," she says, not looking away from me. "We're shopping this aft. We need new bikinis for the party."

All the word shortening is hard to follow, but I caught how she said *new*.

"Okay," says Brianna, nodding. She looks at me. "My mom's picking us up outside after she runs a few errands. Eden says I need something cuter. Do you guys wanna come? We're driving to Northridge."

That's the fancy town next to ours. Ronan would never want to do that, and I don't really have the money to buy anything.

My shoulders droop as I shake my head. I thought Brianna would come over after ice cream and we'd hang out for the day. "We have to get back home," I say. "But thanks."

"I hate that your *mom* has to drive us around," says Eden. "I can't wait till we have our own cars."

She talks like that's happening soon. I don't get this girl.

Eden drops her shades down over her eyes as she scoots out of the booth. "Bye, Ronan," she says with a smile. Then she looks at me. "Bye."

She doesn't use my name, which annoys me because it seems like she did that on purpose.

Brianna gives me a shrug, like she's aware Eden is being weird, as she stands up to follow her cousin. She waves as they walk to the door. And that's when I see Eden catch Ronan's eye and press her lips together into a single kiss.

Really?

When they leave, the bell above the door makes a sound that tinkles like Eden's laugh.

"Whoa."

"Yeah," says Ronan, and that's how I realize I said *whoa* out loud.

"Eden's . . . different this year," I say.

Ronan just stands up and tosses his pile of napkins and the paper from his cone.

"Let's go," he says. "I see the bus."

Chapter 8

It's funny how, in the summer, a weekend can blend in with the regular old weekdays.

"I forgot it was Sunday," I tell Mom when I join her on the couch in front of the TV to watch the morning news show we love that feels like it's from the olden days but still talks about new things.

I curl up beside her and she rests her hand on my head and I breathe her in. On Sunday mornings, she smells the most like herself, without other people's house scents all over her. Ivory soap and sleepiness under a soft cotton nightgown.

"It's a luxury to forget what day it is, Claire," says

Mom. "I'm glad it happens for you."

"Sunday's my favorite," I tell her, because it's my day with her.

After the show we go to a few yard sales around town and Mom looks for treasures, like more puzzles she'll glue together and frame. Puzzles are a real risk at yard sales—more often than not they're missing a piece, even if people put a sign on the box that says All Pieces Here. I don't think they're lying, exactly, I just think they're not sure and they want to make a sale. But boy does it drive Mom crazy to get a puzzle that's missing a piece. That's why I'm so glad I found the blue flower piece last week. In Mom's eyes, that may be the best thing I do all summer.

She finds a seven-hundred-piece waterfall scene that she says reminds her of a hike she went on with her mom and dad. My grandparents both died when I was really little, but Mom has good stories about them and there are photos up in our house, so I try to remember them even if my memories are part imaginary.

I don't mention Eden all day, but I keep picturing the way her pink frosted lips formed into a kiss shape at Ronan. Finally, right when we're about to get back to our neighborhood, something sneaks out. "Brianna's cousin Eden is in town," I say.

"Oh, right," says Mom. "Is she staying for the summer?"

"Yeah."

"You get along with her, don't you?" asks Mom as she takes a left into Twin Pines.

"I don't know," I say, mumbling a little. But then I can't hold it in. "She seems older than thirteen. She's shopping for bikinis with Brianna and she talks about getting a car and she wears a lot of makeup and she's the one who planned the girl-boy pool party."

I don't mention the kissy face at Ronan, and I'm trying to give Mom a list of bad things about Eden, but when I hear the things out loud they don't seem too terrible.

"That sounds like thirteen to me," says Mom as she pulls into our pine-needle-covered parking spot.

"Well, I think she's not *quite* thirteen," I say, pouting.

Mom turns off the engine and puts her hand under my chin. "Hey, this girl really rattled you, didn't she?"

I frown. It's annoying that Eden "rattled" me.

"Are you nervous about the pool party?" Mom asks, which is also annoying because *no*. I hang out with boys all the time. Well, if Ronan counts.

"Forget it," I say. "You had to be there. I'm just saying she seems like trouble."

"Hey, Claire," says Mom, sitting back but not opening her door yet. "What's our motto?"

I sigh. "We may know other people's bathrooms, but we don't know their real stories." It's a cleaning lady thing Mom learned.

"Right."

"But she was bragging about how she hangs out with famous people in Nashville and—"

"Do I need to find you something to do this summer?" asks Mom. "Maybe come to work with me or figure out a way to sign up for a few days of camp? I'm sure it's not too late."

I shut my mouth and shake my head. "No, Mom."

"Boredom sometimes makes small things seem more dramatic," says Mom.

I nod. "Okay," I say. I don't want to risk losing my entire free summer just because some girl was wearing eyeliner and frosted pink lipstick.

In the evening, while Mom is making dinner, I tell her I'm going for a walk. She knows that's code for getting online, since I have to go up to Cleland Cemetery for a good signal, but it's also not a lie: I'm *walking* up there.

I peek over at Ronan's trailer. The main door is open to let a breeze in through the screen, and I see the flicker of the TV in the living room. I'm pretty sure Mr. Michaels's shadow is in its usual spot. I haven't seen him outside since that morning when he was zombie-shuffling. I wonder if he only moves to go to the bathroom. Weird.

I wave to Mrs. Gonzalez when I walk past her trailer. She's leaning on her porch rail, smiling and talking to Mr. Brewster, who's smiling and leaning on his rail too. I notice that Mrs. Gonzalez's thick bun is looser than usual, lower in the back. There are a few gray-black strands falling around her tan face, and it makes me wonder if she's younger than I thought. Maybe even the same age as Mr. Brewster, who has strong arms and a thick beard that's mostly still brown. He wears plaid shirts with the sleeves cut off and his pants have cargo pockets that always look full. He jingles when he walks. I wave to him too, and he raises his soda can in my direction.

See, if we had bigger porches they could sit together.

When I get to the top of the hill and see three bars on my phone, I sit down by the oak tree and open the app I'm not supposed to have to search for *Nash_Queen*. I find her right away, because her profile photo is all pretty hair and sunglasses, and—whoa—she has, like, a thousand followers. Also, she's the first kid I've seen whose profile isn't private. Of course.

I click through to see a few of her photos bigger. There's a selfie with a brunette playing a guitar in the background, and from the comments—there are, like, fifty—I can tell it's some famous country singer. Lots of "omg so jel" stuff is written, and for some reason I'm loading all of them, trying to peek into Eden's social life.

After twenty minutes I feel a little queasy, and I click back to Eden's main page to find her start date. February. I remember how she told Brianna *Everything changes in seventh grade.*

Chapter 9

The gourmet cooking store is empty on a Tuesday. Ronan and I took the bus to the mall this morning, and we plan to spend the whole day inside. I can't always get him to come here with me, but today it's nearly a hundred degrees and the mall has really good air conditioning.

We go to the cooking store first. They do lots of demonstrations, and today's free samples include a raspberry-mango smoothie made by a very shiny blender, fresh guacamole crushed in a black-stone bowl that costs forty dollars, and some crackers that have herbs baked into them. Not bad for a late-morning snack.

"Brianna will be sad she missed the smoothie," I say. When Brianna and I come to the mall, we mostly do the fancy dresses thing and sample makeup. Well, she samples, and I look at all the color names to pick favorites. Currently holding the top spot: Essie's *Roarr-rrange* nail polish. But I texted Brianna a *You free today?* this morning, and she hasn't replied, so it's just me and Ronan. The mall has a different vibe with him, but it's not bad.

When we finish snacking, we stroll past the toy store we used to spend hours in. It has a giant train track, complete with tiny village houses and little people, in the center. We both slow our walk. Then we smile at each other.

"Should we?" I ask. It seems silly to go play with toys when we're eleven, but Ronan's grin tells me he's as into it as I am.

While I make the bridge higher and arrange more complex signals for the train to pass through, Ronan reorganizes the people. Little kids have fun with this setup, but often the firefighters end up at the schoolhouse instead of near their truck, and the tiny dog gets separated from its owner, things like that. So Ronan puts the people and village structures in their rightful places. Technically we're not playing, but getting things back in order.

"They should pay us to do this," Ronan says as he sits the lifeguard into her little raised bench by the lake area. "That would be the greatest job."

"The greatest job is naming makeup colors," I say, flashing to Eden and her rosy lips again. *Pink Peeve.*

"Not for me!" says Ronan, laughing.

"Hey, what did you think of Eden?" I ask Ronan before I lose my nerve. I have to admit that I'd be happy if he said he thought she was snobby or annoying. But instead he says, "She seems cool this year." And he gets this look on his face like he's entering a dream or something.

I purposely drop a heavy track from the bridge I'm working on, and the crash makes him snap out of it. Then I change the subject.

"So is your dad into gardening?" I say. Because I saw him outside again, poking at the dirt bed near their trailer, and I wondered if maybe he was going to plant something like Mrs. Gonzalez has.

Ronan shrugs and doesn't look at me, and I know that means I shouldn't ask more, but Mr. Michaels has been home for a while now and Ronan hasn't said anything at all about how it is to have his dad back.

"Do you think you guys will go to the lake this summer?" I ask, because I remember that being a thing that Ronan and his dad sometimes did when Ronan was little. Before Mr. Michaels left.

I watch Ronan lift up a small kitten piece from the back of a train car and place it in the basket next to the mother cat figure. He shrugs but he doesn't answer out loud. So I stop asking questions.

After we finish with the train set—all pieces safe in their proper spots and tracks fully functional—we wave to the lady at the counter, and I say, "Thanks for letting us play!"

"That's what it's there for!" she says, not seeming to notice that we're almost twelve and not six. Sometimes grown-ups have no idea how old kids are.

Next, we hit this gift store called Quirk, and it's the

perfect place to shake off the serious quiet that happened. I read the funny greeting cards and copy down lines from a few of the best ones in my notebook, which is the only way I ever steal. Who wants to spend five dollars on a card when you can make your own and adults think that's even better? But I can always use help with my messages.

"Booolah!" Ronan comes around the corner wearing crazy, bloodshot googly eyes and makes me jump and then crack up laughing. His fake eyeballs hang from the joke glasses, bouncing up and down on slinky springs.

"Stop plagiarizing," he says when he sees my notebook.

"I'm being resourceful and thrifty," I tell him.

"Well, on my birthday I want a card with words by you, not"—he turns over the back of the card I'm looking at—"American Greetings."

"Fine, fine," I tell him. "I promise you'll get an original Claire Ladd."

He nods, satisfied, and we walk out to the center of the mall where there's a stand selling sunglasses. I think about Brianna's pool party, and I decide I need some. I try on a few frame shapes and settle on a heart-shaped pair with pink around the edges. They're cute, and Ronan says he likes them. Plus, they're in the five-dollar bin. Score!

After I buy them, Ronan puts his hand into his pocket and makes a jingly sound. "Lions?"

"Lions."

We walk to the middle of the mall, where there's a small pool with a fountain that pours out of the mouths of two lion statues that look like they're having a spitting contest. I think they're supposed to look fierce, or maybe regal, but to me they look a little silly. Anyway, we've been wishing in it since we were tiny. Ronan hands me two pennies.

"How many did you bring?" I ask him.

"Three," he says. "It's all I could find in the couch. I think my dad's been cleaning it out."

Usually Ronan recovers at least ten coins from between the cushions. I never bring anything, because Mom puts all her spare change in a jar in the kitchen and I don't like to dip into it. Ronan's couch money has always felt more takable.

I'm about to close my eyes and make a wish when I look at Ronan's face and see his expression change. He's staring over my shoulder with a strange smile.

When I turn, I see Justin Alonzo and Daniel Jacobson from school, but I quickly face Ronan again because I don't want to say hi. Daniel used to flick Brianna's elbow last year in math until he got in trouble, and since then he's been rude to both of us because we told on him. But seriously, if someone is flicking you all the time and you've already asked him to stop and he doesn't, what choice do you have? The thing about flicking is that it's a tiny movement that's not noticeable to teachers, but it can really hurt. So it's like the perfect secret-bully move. That's who Daniel Jacobson is. A secret bully. Justin has never seemed that bad, but he's always with Daniel, so that makes him guilty by friendship.

Ronan's unfamiliar smile gets even bigger. "Hey, guys!" he says in a loud voice.

I turn again, and I spot Emily Wu and Gwen Forester walking with Daniel and Justin. *What is Ronan doing?* They're all popular in our grade. We've known them forever, of course, and I don't really understand how suddenly some people seem more famous at school than others, but that has definitely happened for this crowd. The girls aren't mean to us or anything, they're just . . . not our people. They see us, but they won't talk to us.

"You guys, hi!" Emily says brightly, coming over to the fountain. *Okay, I was wrong.* The rest of them follow, and Justin and Daniel give Ronan head nods like boys do.

Emily talks fast and moves her hands a lot. Ronan and I both lean back slightly to make room for her gestures. She's standing close. "How are your summers so far?" she asks. And before either of us can answer she says, "Ronan, I just found you online. You finally have a profile."

Ronan laughs. "I know, right? *Finally.*"

I squint at his face. His voice sounds weird. Clear and crisp and loud.

Gwen and Emily turn to me then. "Are you guys, like, here *together?*" Gwen asks.

"I mean, we're both here," I say. I know what she means, but it's an annoying question. At the same time, Ronan says, "*Nonono*, just hanging out."

"So are you coming to the movies?" asks Emily.

"What?" I ask.

"I thought maybe Brianna texted you," she says. "Oh, there she is!"

I turn again and see Brianna and Eden striding toward us, and a small, sharp pain stabs my stomach. I zero in on Brianna, blocking out the rest of the mall, because in a flash, like milliseconds, I put it together that my best friend is meeting spinning-top Emily and Gwen and Justin and Daniel-the-Flicker to go to the movies and she didn't invite *me*! I think I see Brianna's face wobble slightly, but then Eden starts talking and it's like a giant spotlight has moved onto her.

"Hey, I'm Brianna's cousin Eden," she says to no one and everyone.

Emily does the introductions, and I notice she's staring up at Eden with an awe I haven't seen from her before, but when she gets around to me and Ronan, Eden says, "We know each other." Then Eden smiles at me and says, "I didn't know you guys were going to be here."

"I think everyone's surprised." I'm looking at Brianna when I talk. Her hair is down again, and I notice she's wearing a new white sundress along with what must be new red ballet flats—I've never seen them. She's also suddenly very interested in the mall's fake marble floors.

Justin's giant sneaker is making a loud noise as he kicks the base of the fountain like he's antsy.

"You guys are cousins?" asks Daniel. "You don't look alike."

"My dad's black," says Eden. She flashes a bright-lipped smile at him, but when he looks away I see her smile drop.

"Guys, let's go," says Emily. "The show starts soon."

"What are you seeing?" asks Ronan, like this is all normal.

"The new Selena Gomez movie," says Eden.

"I love her," both Gwen and Emily say at once, as Justin and Daniel grunt. If they don't want to go to the movie, why are they even here?

"Want to come with?" Gwen's looking at Ronan.

"Sorry, can't," he says, but he doesn't say why. We counted our money earlier, and we plan to split a slice of pizza for lunch after we make wishes in the fountain.

"Too bad," says Eden, and she pouts a little. Her lips are more orangy today. *Cruel Coral.*

Gwen's still looking at Ronan when she says, "But you'll be at Brianna's party, right?"

And that is when my jaw finally drops. *How big is this birthday party?*

Brianna must know what I'm thinking because this time when I look over at her, she meets my eyes and gives me a cringing smile. The little stabbing pain in my stomach gets more intense.

"Definitely, I'll be there," says Ronan. Like I'm not even here.

"Cool, see you soon then," says Emily, and I hear Brianna say a quiet "bye," but her back is already turning to me, joining the crowd of six who are walking away from us, toward the movie theater.

I open my palm and realize that I've been gripping my pennies crazy hard—they made indentations in my palm. I fling them both into the fountain without even making a wish.

Chapter 10

My dad picks us up from the mall. He texted to say he got off work early and he checked in with Mom about taking me out to dinner. I told him Ronan was with me, and he got that I meant we'll all be doing dinner together.

I'm extra glad, because I don't want to think about Brianna anymore and my dad is the kind of fun that usually makes me forget bad feelings.

The three of us hit a fast-food place, and I almost order the kiddie meal with the toy because they're featuring some of my favorite characters right now, but when Ronan goes for a regular-size combo I decide to too. What will I do with the toys anyway?

"You been to any baseball games this year, Ronan?" asks my dad when we sit down in our booth. Minor League Baseball is a big thing in our area, and sometimes Ronan's mom gets tickets.

"No, sir," says Ronan. "Mom's working a lot."

"Well, maybe your father will take you now that he's home," says my dad, and I tense up a little because I'm not sure how Ronan will react.

"Maybe," says Ronan, concentrating hard on his burger.

Dad quickly speaks again. "Or I will! I'd love to see a game with you. Claire always gets bored by the fourth inning and wants to leave."

"Dad!" I protest.

"It's true, Clairebear," he says. "Popcorn gets you through the first inning, then a hot dog, then cotton candy, and you're done. My wallet is flat as a pancake and I don't even get to see half the game!"

Ronan looks at me and cracks a smile.

"Well, it takes so long for them to play," I say, grinning back at him. "Just finish already!"

"She's more a basketball fan," says Ronan to my dad. It's true.

"That she is, Ronan, that she is." Dad ruffles my hair, and I'm glad to be here with them right now, and glad that Dad knew how to make a joke and fix the bad feeling that was at the table for a minute, the one that had to do with Mr. Michaels.

But when we get back to Twin Pines and he's dropping us off, Dad says, "Claire, I'm going to be out of town next Friday. Ask your mom if we can switch and I can see you on Sunday?" He smiles and winks at me. "We'll go fishing, okay?"

I scowl at him. "Why can't you talk to her?"

"I've got to get home," he says, still smiling. "I'll text her later to confirm, but can you just let her know we need to switch days?"

"Fine." I close Charlie's door extra hard and it slams.

Ronan raises his eyebrows at me as Dad drives away.

"I know," I say. "It's like they expect me to go between them all the time. Why can't they just talk to each other?"

I wait for Ronan to agree with me, but he doesn't

move, and he doesn't say anything.

"What?" I ask him, because he's still staring at me and now his eyes are squinting a little, like maybe in a judging way.

"Anyway," he says. Again, like that means something. He doesn't get it; his parents don't relay messages through him like he's an assistant schedule-maker or something.

I huff at him and go inside where Mom is waiting.

The texts come in all at once that night as I'm brushing my teeth.

Brianna: i didn't see your text this morning

Brianna: emily texted me last minute about the movies

Brianna: i know you don't really like to go to movies

(Not true, but she's right that I don't go often.)

Brianna: i think she only invited me because she got my party invitation

Brianna: also my mom is becoming friends with her mom because we live near them now

Brianna: eden says having a big party will make it more fun and my mom thinks so too

Brianna: want to come over tomorrow to swim? the pool is finally ready!

Brianna: are you mad? please don't be mad

Brianna: text me when you get these

She knows that my phone sometimes doesn't deliver texts right away because of the signal problems in Twin Pines Park. I read all these texts while I brush my teeth for a full minute. Mom keeps a plastic hourglass timer that we got at the dentist on the sink so I'll know how long to brush. I rinse my toothbrush, fill a cup with water, swish, and spit.

Then I take my phone into my room and get under the covers. I don't want to answer Brianna right away, because I've had that stabby pain in my stomach since I saw her at the mall, and I want her to feel it too.

I wonder when she originally sent the texts. I picture her feeling anxious all day. It's nine p.m. now. Is that enough worrying for her? I do want to go swimming tomorrow.

And I guess it makes sense that Emily invited Brianna to the movies after getting the pool party invitation. But are they friends now?

Claire: Fine. I'll come swimming.

Chapter 11

The next morning at ten a.m., there's a knock on my door.

I open it and am surprised to see Brianna and Eden outside—I didn't hear anyone drive up. But I peek around them and there's Brianna's mom in a little silver car. I wave to her. "Wow, that thing is quiet."

"It's new," says Eden. "It's a Prius. Everyone in Nashville has them—they're eco friendly."

"Oh," I say. "Cool." I promised my mom I'd give Eden "the benefit of the doubt," and besides, I'm not mad at her for not being invited to the movies. I'm still a little mad at Brianna, honestly, but I also really want to swim.

I put up a finger. "I'll go get my bag!"

I turn and head into my room to grab the backpack I stuffed with my new swimsuit and my favorite flowered towel. When I get back to the living room, Eden and Brianna are both standing inside the door.

"I've never been in . . . one of these," says Eden. Then she smiles and a little laugh escapes her frosty lips. They're *Pink Peeve* again. "It's almost like one long room."

I look around my trailer and see the tiny tray Mom put next to the door for keys and the phone so we'd have an entry. And the way she angled the two chairs at our small folding table to make something like a dining area. Things are neat and clean, just the way Mom and I like them.

But then I watch Eden's face as her eyes move around. She's looking at the peeling linoleum spot on the kitchen counter, the small coffee stain on the rug under the TV stand that Mom can't seem to get out, even with lots of scrubbing. Eden shifts her weight and there's a slight creak, and I think about how the floor sometimes feels a little lumpy under our feet.

Brianna's just standing there.

"So, if you wanted to," continues Eden, "could you, like, travel in this? Like if you hooked it up to a car?"

I tilt my head. "What?"

She grins and waves her hand at me. "Never mind," she says. "That was probably a dumb question. Sorry, first time in a trailer."

"It's okay," I say automatically.

"Let's go, you guys," says Brianna. She holds the door open as Eden and then I walk outside to the silent car.

"Sorry again," Brianna whispers as Eden walks ahead. I know she means about yesterday.

"It's okay," I say, deciding to let her off the hook. "I didn't want to see that movie anyway."

Brianna and I sit in back while Eden takes the front seat with Brianna's mom, who asks how I am and then about my mom. Thankfully she's happy with one-word answers.

It only takes five minutes to get to Brianna's house.

It's so close that I could probably walk if I felt like it, but it does involve a major road, so it wouldn't be, like, a nice stroll or anything.

We have a few still moments in the car, though, and I look out the window and squint at the bright morning sun. I think about what Eden said about my home, and I can feel something that hurts, like, physically, in my chest.

And the hurt takes me by surprise because I know most people live in houses and not trailers. But I've always liked my home, and I've never been bothered by trailer park jokes or whatever. I've heard them.

But I guess it's different . . . hearing random comments and jokes out in the world versus hearing someone who's standing inside your living room saying something.

I take a deep breath, which is a thing we learned in preschool but that still works for strong feelings. I focus on the fact that soon I'll be swimming, splashing around with Brianna in the heat.

I look over and smile at Brianna as a square of hot

sunlight settles in between us on the back seat. I really am excited about her pool. She grins back, and I exhale some of the bad feeling.

At Brianna's new house, there are lots of trees out front and a long driveway, so you can't see much from the street. When we get close, though, I feel my breathing slow a little because . . . it's big. Not like a mansion, I guess, but way bigger than the house she had before, which I always thought was extra special because it had a living room that was only for sitting and talking—the TV was in a "den." But I bet this house has, like, three dens.

"Tour!" shouts Eden when we walk in through the big double doors, and Brianna looks at me, shrugging.

"Do you want to see . . . ? I mean, we don't have to—"

"No, sure!" I say enthusiastically. "Show me your room!"

"Shoes, please," says Mrs. Foley. Once we've kicked them off, she says, "I'll go make some refreshments."

Then Eden takes over and leads me all around the house: to the home office with dark wood shelves, to the den with a real light-up jukebox, to the fancy living room that has one wall of all windows that look out on the woods. We go upstairs to see five bedrooms, plus four bathrooms, all with sparkly clean tubs that shoot whirlpool jets—one has a huge skylight too.

"This is so cool," I tell Brianna, and it is. She smiles at me but doesn't say anything.

"I know, right?" Eden responds like it's her house.

We end up in Brianna's room. "Isn't it pretty?" says Eden.

Beautiful is more the word for it, with its lacy curtains and pale-pink walls and flowered rug. But the best part is the window, which sits inside a big archway. There's a pastel polka-dot pillow there, and I imagine Brianna might curl up on it and read or listen to music while she looks out at the trees.

The window in my room, the one I look out to see Mrs. Gonzalez's wildflowers, suddenly seems really small.

"Now we'll show you the basement," says Eden. "It's—

"No, that's enough!" interrupts Brianna. "She can see it later. Let's change into bathing suits!" She claps her hands to officially end the tour. And I'm relieved.

Brianna's mom pours us watermelon juice, which I didn't even know was a thing you could have, but it's really good and she serves it in glasses that are frosty cold and we get to sit around the pool in reclining lounge chairs like we're famous. There's a fluffy towel on each chair and extras in the corner in baskets, so I didn't even need to bring mine.

Eden and Brianna wear loose-fitting dresses that Eden calls "cover-ups" so they look like Hollywood stars. I just have my cutoffs and tank top, but I'm glad I got the new bikini from Gemma. It fits like I bought it for myself.

I finish my pink juice and strip down to my suit. "Let's get in!" I shout. Then I pencil-jump straight into the deep end of the pool.

The water is cool and refreshing, with that chlorine smell that reminds me of vacations. Mom and I stayed at a motel with a pool in Florida two summers ago when we went to visit her aunt and uncle. I keep my head submerged for a beat because I love the heavy silence that only happens underwater. Then I kick my feet and a string of bubbles comes out of my nose as I rush up to break the surface.

I smooth my hair back and swim to the side of the pool, pulling my upper half out and resting my elbows on the stone edge with my feet hanging in the water. Even the ground around the pool is nice. It's not rough concrete like the pool area at the apartment complex where my dad lives—it's smooth and white. Maybe marble! I think about the arched window and the jetstream bathtubs and this deep-blue pool, and I guess that Brianna is rich now.

"Cute suit," says Brianna, and I'm glad she likes it. She starts to put her arms up to take off her flowy dress.

"Wait, Bri—" Eden reaches into a small basket on the round table next to her lounge chair and holds up two bottles of nail polish—a blue and a gold. She flips them over and looks at the bottoms. *"True Blue or All That Glitters?"*

"All that glitters isn't gold," I whisper, working out the expression in my head. I think it means flashy things aren't always special on the inside. I say it loud—"gold"—even though she didn't ask me, because I think it fits Eden.

Eden raises an eyebrow at me, but then she nods and hands the bottle to Brianna, who puts her arms down again and sits back on the chair.

"You guys, come swim!" I say. "We can paint our nails later."

Eden ignores me, but Brianna looks over and bites her lip. "I promised Eden I would do hers," she says. "I'll be quick."

"Whatever." I whisper it as I push back into the pool. I don't even feel that mad. I mean, really, *whatever.* I'm in a pool, and I'm gonna enjoy it.

I lie back and float in "starfish" which is a move we all learned in YMCA swim lessons when we were four.

When I lift my head back up a couple of minutes

later, Brianna is about to do a cannonball right on top of me, and I scream-laugh, paddling out of the way as she splashes into the middle of the deep end.

"Bri!" Eden shrieks as a wave of water surges out of the pool and onto her outstretched legs. She holds her hands up in the air in mock horror. "These are drying!"

On second thought, maybe her horror is real. She doesn't seem like she can take a joke.

"Sorry," says Brianna, and she sounds sincere, but then she turns away from Eden and smiles at me. I sense an eye roll even though she doesn't actually do it, and I'm happy that she chose the pool over painting her own nails. "Silly jumps?" she asks.

"Yes!"

We play this game whenever we're in a pool—one of us describes a person or animal and the other jumps into the pool as that character.

"Charlie Chaplin with his cane," I say. We used to watch this old comedian, maybe he was even the first comedian ever, in short videos online. Brianna does a little penguin waddle and pretends to twirl a cane in the air as she jumps in, toes splayed with heels together in a signature Charlie move.

"A dolphin who can talk," says Brianna as she climbs the ladder out of the pool, and when I jump in I jerk my head and shout, "I'm a mammal!" She's laughing when I pop up.

Then I hear Eden's shriek, so loud it's like a scream, above Brianna's laugh. "Oh, this boy!"

"Who?" asks Brianna, walking close and leaning over Eden's shoulder.

"Ronan," says Eden, eyes on me as she raises her sunglasses. I climb out of the pool and walk toward her. Then I peer over her other shoulder and she leans away from my dripping hair.

I'm looking at a selfie of Ronan. He has his fishing rod in one hand, and he's holding the camera up at an angle so you can see the green leaves of the trees and the rippling water behind him. There's a ray of sun crossing his hair, and I notice all the gold in it again.

The caption reads, *Perfect day at the lake.*

The lake? That's definitely the brook. Right? I look more closely. Could it be the lake? How would Ronan get there? But then I realize I'm sure it's the brook because I see our rock in the corner of the frame.

"He is gonna be *cu-u-ute*," says Eden, scrolling away from the image.

"He's Ronan," says Brianna, shrugging in this way like, *How could we look at him like that?*

"Wait till the pool party, B," says Eden. Then she shakes her head. "I can't believe you were thinking about just girls."

"Either way would be fun," I say, standing up for Brianna. The party should be what she wants it to be—it's her birthday.

Eden rolls her eyes before she pulls down her sunglasses. I don't know how long I can give her the benefit of the doubt. I head back to the edge of the water.

Why is Ronan lying online? And what phone did he use to take that picture, anyway? My mind is spinning with silent questions.

Brianna breaks my thoughts by grabbing my hand and jumping into the pool, pulling me with her. "Sneak attack!" she says when we both come up smiling.

I splash her, and she shrieks and swims away.

"You know what we need?" she says from the

shallow end. "A slide like at your dad's place."

I laugh. Every so often Brianna comes with me to Dad's apartment—once she even spent the night—and the pool there has this twisty waterslide, but it's ancient and rickety and on hot days your butt sticks to it and doesn't let you move at all. Plus the pool itself gets kind of janky. We have to use the scooper thing for clumps of leaves and dead wasps. This pool is perfect.

"Your dad has a pool?" asks Eden, sitting up in her chair.

"There's one at his apartment complex," I say.

"Oh." She reclines again.

"It's so much fun and bigger than this one," says Brianna, and I smile at her, thinking about how we have spent entire days swimming over at Dad's. I guess we won't do that anymore, now that she has her own pool.

We do a few more rounds of silly jumps. I suggest a jack-in-the-box, and then a grumpy gorilla and a venus flytrap. For that one, I find a fallen leafy branch by the edge of the pool and pass it to Brianna as she jumps in so she can snap her trap shut midjump.

Brianna has me do a dog with three legs and a

pirate's parrot and then a runway model.

For that one, I back up to the fence and start a long, strutting walk with a hand on my waist. I put one foot in front of the other with exaggerated hip swishes and an upturned snobby chin. I keep going until I fall right into the pool in a perfect toe-point jump.

"Extra points for the small splash!" says Brianna when I emerge and climb up the ladder. "Models definitely aren't big splashers."

"You guys have to see this," says Eden from her chair.

"What?" I ask, shaking out my hair as I grab my towel. I'm ready to take a break and dry off.

She laughs and waves me over. Her golden nails flash in the sun. "It's Daniel and Justin—they're so funny!"

I look over her shoulder again and see that Justin posted a photo of the two of them on some fishing boat. Justin is holding up a big fish, and Daniel is pretending to kiss its lips.

I hear myself laugh but it doesn't sound like me. I don't really think the picture is that clever. And why is

Eden following them now? She's suddenly best friends with everyone here?

She starts typing a comment and leans toward Brianna, showing her the screen. They both laugh, but Eden has her hand covering the side near me—I can't see what she wrote.

I decide that instead of sitting by the side of the pool with Eden, I'd rather jump back in. So I do. I toss the towel aside and dive straight into the deep end. I dive with so much determination and force, in fact, that my face hits the bottom of the pool.

Hard.

Chapter 12

I can tell right away that it's bad, not so much by the pain, which is sharp, but by the cloud of red blood that blooms in the water in front of me as I open my eyes. And when I come up, I must look like a horror movie because Brianna's eyes go huge and Eden starts screaming.

That brings Brianna's mom outside, and when she sees me she drops her frosted watermelon-juice glass. It crashes to the ground and breaks into pieces.

"Claire, honey, out of the pool," she says, ignoring the glass and grabbing a towel from the fluffy stack near the deck. She rushes over to me. "Brianna, go get some ice from inside."

Then Mrs. Foley has her arm around me, and she's wrapping a towel over my shoulders and leading me to a seat under the sun umbrella. "Let's see," she says, wiping at the top of my nose with a second towel—*ouch*. Brianna runs up with an ice pack, and her mom wraps the towel around it and brings it to the space between my eyes. She presses gently.

"Does it hurt?" asks Brianna.

I nod. "It's not awful though," I say, and that's true. I mean, I definitely whacked my face on the bottom of the pool—I think I probably hit the curve where the deep end becomes the shallow end—but there's so much blood that it looks worse than it is. At least I hope it does.

When Brianna's mom takes away the towel it's soaked in red. "Sweetie, I think you really rammed your nose there," she says. She puts her fingers under my chin and turns my head from side to side to inspect me from different angles. "There's a cut on the top. It's not broken, though," she says. "You'd know if it was."

"A surface wound," I say. My dad says when you

hurt your head it bleeds a ton because there are lots of blood vessels close to the skin there. "Nothing to worry about. The towel, though. I'm sorry it—"

"Oh, the cleaning lady will get it, don't worry," says Mrs. Foley. "I just want to be sure you're all right."

I nod and swallow hard. "Really," I say. "I'm fine. We can keep swimming."

Brianna's mom clucks her tongue. "I don't think so," she says. "Claire, I'm going to have to call your mom— she should know what happened."

"Don't, Mrs. Foley," I plead. "She's working, and she can't come get me. Really, I'll be okay." Then I think maybe they don't want me in the water because of the blood. "I'll stay out of the pool, I was done swimming anyway."

Brianna's mom smiles at me. "Okay, I won't insist that your mom come get you, but I'm going to give her a call for the heads-up anyway. And you promise to let me know if it starts hurting more."

"I will," I say.

"Keep this on it." Brianna's mom hands the ice back

to me after she wraps it in a fresh towel. "It'll help control the swelling."

I nod. "Thanks."

She goes inside with the bloody towel, and I lean against the soft yellow-striped pillow of the chair. I close my eyes.

"Maybe we should dry off and watch a movie," says Brianna.

"What? I didn't even get to swim yet," says Eden.

I keep my eyes closed because if I didn't they would roll all the way up into my head. If it were up to me, Brianna and I would go inside and Eden would stay out here. Forever.

Brianna's voice goes all singsongy. "We can watch the newest *Star Girls.*"

I open my eyes. That movie was just in theaters, like, a month ago.

Brianna looks at me. "My parents got some TV package where almost everything is on demand now," she explains like it's no big deal.

And then we go inside and they take me down a

set of stairs that weren't part of the tour. When Eden said "basement," I pictured a cobwebby space filled with boxes. But no. This place is all white walls and soft blue carpet. The big room is set up like a movie theater, and the screen takes up almost the whole wall. There are two speakers on either side of it, and a big, comfy, U-shaped couch, so we each get a long space to stretch out on.

"Wow" is all I can say. It comes out kind of whispery.

Brianna grabs the remote and finds the movie right away. Then she puts in a password and, voilà, we are watching the new *Star Girls*.

When her mom comes down and says, "Are you girls ready to order pizza?" Brianna shushes her while nodding.

I find myself half watching the movie and half watching Brianna and Eden. What they laugh at, how they look back and forth at each other. Brianna looks at me sometimes too, it's not like she's ignoring me. But something feels off. She doesn't ask about my nose, even though I keep adjusting the ice pack.

Is it because of this new house? The pool? Or is it because Eden is here with her dazzling curls and her fancy cover-up and gold nails? I had fun swimming with Brianna, but Eden scrolling through her phone really put me in a bad mood.

A little while later, Mrs. Foley brings down a large pizza with extra cheese and a two-liter bottle of soda, plus garlic knots and dipping sauces. Eden and Brianna don't turn away from the screen, but I make sure to whisper, "Thank you."

"You're welcome, Claire," she says quietly. Then she hands me a new ice pack and mouths, "You okay?" I give her a thumbs-up sign and hand her the old pack. I put the new one on my nose, but when she leaves I take it off. My face doesn't hurt much anymore.

I fill up on pizza and garlic knots, plus three glasses of soda, before the movie ends. When the credits roll, I stretch and yawn, and I see Eden staring at me.

"Your face is so messed up," she says.

"Ooh, Claire, does it still hurt?" Brianna chimes in.

"A little." The ice pack was cold but it did make my nose feel better. I stand up to go into the bathroom, and when I turn on the light and look in the mirror, I see what they're saying.

There's a black-and-blue ring forming under my left eye, and my nose itself has a bright-red cut right at the top. It's not even a place where any shape of Band-Aid could fit, so I guess I have to walk around like this. Unless I want to put a paper bag over my head.

I splash some water onto my cheeks and then I smile at myself in the mirror. I can laugh this off.

"I guess I need a paper bag to wear over my head," I say when I walk out, and Brianna laughs but Eden kind of cringes and nods, like she really thinks that would help.

Later when they drop me off, I promise Mrs. Foley that I'll ice my nose some more tonight and that I'll give her best to my mom. Then I wave good-bye to all of them but before I can leave the back seat, Brianna tries to hug me. I give her a half hug and pull away.

Inside my living room, I unload my backpack and take a deep breath as I look around. At the flowered couch covered with a knit blanket my mom's mom, Grandma Lou, made when I was born. At the window in the kitchen, small and round—the only round window I've seen in Twin Pines Park, which always made it feel extra special. At the bright-red toaster Mom bought last summer for "a pop of color" while she saves up for one of those heavy ceramic pots that come in bright shades. At the narrow hallway that's lined with Mom's framed puzzles and photos of our family, including one of me, Mom, and Dad when I was first born. The hall leads to the bathroom, with its bright-blue tub, and two bedrooms—the perfect size for Mom and me. It's always been our home.

But right now, in this moment, it doesn't feel special at all.

Chapter 13

The sun is setting by the time I spot Ronan walking toward his trailer. No one answered when I knocked earlier, but I thought I saw Mr. Michaels slumped on the couch. It's weird how he doesn't come to the door, but honestly, if Ronan's not home I don't want to have to talk to his dad. So I walked around and checked out Mrs. Gonzalez's garden instead. The tomatoes were still pretty green, but I could see tinges of red starting to spread. There was a new low fence around her plot too, and I noticed that it was the same style as the pen Mr. Brewster built for Rocky—sturdy and nice looking, made from dark wood.

I need to talk to Ronan. While I was waiting, I kept thinking about the time this winter when Mom and I drove some girls home after basketball practice. In the back seat, Josephine Pritchard whispered a joke about all the cleaning supplies in my mom's car, and I heard. But I didn't get upset. I turned around and said, "I'm not embarrassed by it. My mom works hard." It was that simple. Josephine didn't say anything more. Mom said that me being okay with me makes other people okay with me, and I've found that to be true.

So why did today with Eden and Brianna feel different? Today, so much about me felt not okay.

I hear a branch snap and look up to see Ronan carrying his fishing rod and a small Styrofoam cooler. Right. The selfie.

Rocky is jogging next to Ronan.

"Hey," I say.

When Ronan looks up, his jaw goes slack. He drops everything in his hands and rushes toward me.

My nose. I forgot.

"Claire, what happened? Who—?"

I put up my hand. "It was the pool," I say.

"What?"

"Brianna's pool. It attacked me. Came right up and took a chunk out of my nose and left me with this black eye too." I smile to show him I'm okay because he still looks upset.

"Must be a pretty tough pool," he says, sounding skeptical. He squints at me. "Are you sure it was just . . ."

"Ronan, it was the pool."

"So that's where you were?" he asks. "At Brianna's?"

"Yeah," I say. "Sorry I didn't tell you." It's not like I have to let Ronan in on all my plans, but maybe me being gone without a word was kind of rude.

He starts walking away. "Doesn't matter," he mumbles.

"Well, let's hang out now," I say, following him. Ronan walks up to Mr. Brewster's trailer to open the dog-pen gate for Rocky. I check to be sure Mr. Brewster's car isn't here and then I say, "Hey, did I tell you that I saw Mrs. Gonzalez and Mr. Brewster leaning over their porch rails to talk to each other the other day? And look at her garden plot!" I point toward the tomatoes. "I think he built that new fence for her."

Ronan shrugs. "So?"

"I don't know," I say, letting my arm drop. "I mean, they're kind of the same age . . . they both live alone . . ."

"You're being gossipy, Claire," he says, locking Rocky's gate and heading back to get his rod and cooler.

"Fine." I sigh loudly and change the subject. I'm stalling because I don't really know how to bring up what I want to talk about. "Did you catch anything?"

"Just some sunfish, which I threw back," he says. "I did get one smallmouth though. It's in here." He taps the cooler, and I nod like I want him to open it up and show me, so he does.

The fish has a green-gold shine to it, and the one eye I can see stares blankly as it lies on the ice. I watch its last breaths going in and out, in and out.

"Close it," I say, turning away. I feel like I'll cry if I keep looking at that fish.

Ronan shuts the cooler.

"How was the pool?" he asks as we head over to my porch steps and sit down side by side. "Aside from the . . ." He gestures at my nose.

"It was . . . weird," I say. Ronan and I are sitting really close together because the steps are narrow, so I look out at a scrawny pine tree between our trailers. If I turned my head I'd be talking pretty much straight into his ear.

"Weird how?" asks Ronan.

I stare at the flecked bark on the ground. Suddenly I feel like maybe telling Ronan all about my feelings is going against Brianna. I could talk to her about it, right? But when I think of actually doing that my stomach clenches. What would I say? "Um, I feel bad that you're rich now and have all these cool things and I don't."

"I don't know . . . ," I start, and Ronan gives me space to keep going. So after a minute, I do. "Have you ever noticed how Brianna has everything? How she *gets* everything?" And once I've said that, I can't stop talking. "I mean, anything that comes into her mind will suddenly materialize in front of her, like she has her own magic genie to answer every wish! She has new jewelry and shoes and two dens and her own bathroom that's just for her and a polka-dot pillow in her window where she can sit and read or be on her phone or whatever. And it's not only the house. First we're out by her pool and then we're watching a brand-new movie on her big TV and having pizza and soda and even garlic knots."

Ronan doesn't say anything. He's looking at his trailer door, which is partly open. I see a flicker of TV light.

I swat his arm. "Hey, you're not listening to me," I say, standing with a stomp of my flip-flop.

"I heard you, Claire," he says, standing up beside me. "But yeah. I mean, duh. I've always known that other kids have things that I don't."

"Doesn't it bother you?" I ask.

"Yes!" he says, his voice a mad whisper as he glances back at his trailer again, and now we're standing here in front of my doorway like we're in a fight. "I'm mad every day that I don't have a different life!"

"Is that why you posted that selfie?" I ask. "'On the lake'? Please, Ronan, you were at the brook. And whose phone did you use, anyway?"

That gets him. "How did you see that?" he asks.

"Eden follows you," I say. "She showed us." Then, because I see the question in his eyes, I say, "Don't worry, I didn't tell them you were lying. But I'm sure Brianna knew."

"Maybe I wish I could get to the lake," he says. "Besides, who cares? It doesn't hurt anyone."

He's jealous. Like I am. But I'm not lying about stuff. "Them being able to go to the lake, and having money . . . it doesn't make them better," I say, thinking about Justin and Daniel's post, and coming back to what I know to be true, what has to be true. I'm saying what I wanted Ronan to say to me. I need to be reassured, but that's not happening.

"Maybe I just wanted to pretend for a minute!" Ronan's voice is quiet but he still sounds mad, like he's boiling under the surface. He picks up his fishing rod and cooler and starts to walk toward his door.

"But the brook is so great," I say, thinking of our cool rock on a hot day. "You don't need to pretend you're somewhere else."

"Maybe *you* don't need to pretend you're somewhere else!" He looks over his shoulder as I follow him. "You don't get to say what I need!"

I feel a tremble coming in my lip, but I hold it still. I will not cry.

We're in front of Ronan's door now, and he turns to look right at me. "I'll tell you what I don't need, Claire. I don't need you telling me how much Brianna has that you don't! You're complaining about her not knowing what *she* has? You have plenty, all right? God, you can be so *stupid* sometimes!"

I'm stunned. It's like he slapped me. I wait for him to take it back, to say he's sorry, to at least soften his face, which looks meaner than I've ever seen it—all hard angles and sunburn.

But he doesn't do any of that. He just opens the screen door and leaves me there.

"Ronan!" I shout. He turns to me, and I open my mouth to . . . I don't know. Stop him, make him understand me.

"You look like a caught fish with that open mouth,

Claire," he says. So I close it again.

And then I turn around to go home, and on my way I kick up the dirt in the raised bed outside Ronan's trailer, which is filled with nothing.

Chapter 14

"Claire, do you have the Lysol?"

"Yeah!" I head downstairs to the kitchen
to bring my mom her can't-do-without cleaning prod-
uct. People like to be fancy and eco friendly, but Mom
always asks if she can use some of her own supplies
for especially hard-to-clean areas. The less harsh stuff
doesn't work as well.

"Put it on the counter, thanks," says Mom, and she
sticks her head back into the oven to fight the grease
of a chicken that got roasted at the Skyler residence.
Even though they're gone for most of the summer, Mr.
Skyler is home a few days a week for work, and he still

wants Mom to "keep things spick-and-span," at least that's what his note on the table says.

When I was little, Mom held me in a carrier as she cleaned, and later she brought a playpen that would fence me into one area. All of her clients welcomed me, because if they didn't, they didn't get Mom as their cleaning person. And she's the best.

When I do a job with her, Mom pays me five dollars an hour, and she has me put the finishing touches on rooms after she's done the deep clean. Right now I'm working on the upstairs hall bath at Gemma's—straightening the hand towels, doing a mirror inspection, rinsing out the soap tray, and adding a new fancy bar that's shaped like a swan.

I lean close to the sparkling-clean mirror to inspect my face. My left eye still has a purple bruise underneath it that's fading to yellow, and my nose is scabbed a bit, right at the top. Mom made a little noise when she first saw it, like it looked worse than she thought it would. Brianna's mom had called her, but I guess she didn't get the full picture. "Does it hurt?" she asked me. And I said *no* truthfully. It really doesn't. Unless I press on it or something. And my sunglasses cover both the eye and the bridge-of-nose issue, so I've got them with me.

It's good to earn a little money, maybe for something I'll need before school. I tell myself that's why I came to work with Mom today. But also, I didn't want to be home when Ronan knocks. If he knocks.

I still don't understand what happened, why he got so mad. I went to him feeling bad about Brianna, but I left our conversation feeling much worse. Like completely upside down. I keep hearing him say, "You can be so *stupid* sometimes!" I thought Ronan would understand how I felt about Brianna's new house. I thought he would be the *only one* who'd understand.

Since the Skylers are gone, I decide to poke around a little bit. When I was younger, Gemma and I would play in the backyard tree house for hours while Mom cleaned. It's big enough to hold a toy kitchen and multiple sets of doll bunk beds, so we usually ended up playing a game we called Restaurant in a Hospital. Gemma's little brother, Sam, mostly uses it now, and when I peeked up there this morning I saw a set of train tracks running across the floor, a Darth Vader poster on one wall, and a cardboard box filled with packages of crackers and cookies in the corner. I smiled at that because Gemma and I were never allowed to eat up there; I've heard that second kids get away with more.

But I didn't come for the tree house. I came for Gemma's room.

I know the oven is going to keep Mom busy for a while, so I walk out of the hall bath and through the next door on the right.

Mom already cleaned Gemma's bedroom—queen-size comforter tight and straight, pillows fluffed, rug vacuumed. A bulletin board, newly dusted, holds drama programs from middle school, pictures of Gemma's friends, birthday cards. She has a TV on one wall with a sleek set of speakers underneath it. Her comforter has a country theme—covered bridges and grassy areas and farmhouses are gathered together in little scenes. I think there's a word for this fabric pattern but I don't remember it.

I've always loved the black-and-white family photos clustered on one wall. In the pictures the Skylers are all dressed in white—on beaches, in front of big houses, even one where they all seem to be on top of a mountain, still completely in white. Or maybe they're wearing pastels and I can't tell because of the black-and-white thing.

The pictures seem like something from a movie—the perfect happy family. At least, that's how I always saw them before. Today, the images aren't making me calm like they used to. I have questions. I look into Gemma's eyes. I want to figure out what she's thinking, which is hard to do with a photo, but I try anyway. Did she know that she was lucky to be at the beach, or skiing, or staying in a big vacation house? Did she care?

I step up to Gemma's vanity—a table with a mirror above it where she puts on makeup and does her hair. On top of the table is a fancy gold tray that holds bottles of perfume. When I pick one up, the others make a nice clinking sound. Princess by Vera Wang. It's my favorite, the prettiest bottle, shaped like a heart with a crown on top. *She won't miss one spray.* I close my eyes and lean my face into a pouf of sweet-smelling air.

I think about Mom with her head in the Skylers' oven.

The damp mist feels good on my face, so I pick up another bottle. Live Colorfully by Kate Spade. I sniff it and put it down again. *Clink.*

I think about Gemma and her black-and-white vacations.

Poppy Citrine Blossom by Coach. *Sniff. Clink.*

I think about Brianna and her new pool and the polka-dot window seat.

Modern Muse by Estée Lauder. *Sniff. Clink.*

I think about Eden and her fancy Nashville life with gold nails and perfect online posts.

Miss Dior by Christian Dior. *Sniff. Clink.*

I think about Ronan and his fake selfie.

I'm in a zone now, picking up bottle after bottle and taking a whiff of each one—I can't tell what smells like what anymore. How can one girl have so much perfume? I spray the next one into the air, and then I spin-step into it. I like the way the scent wafts when I move, and I linger in the perfume cloud, thinking about the weeds outside my window that I like to pretend are wildflowers. Thinking about Ronan's dad's dirty couch spot and vacant eyes.

A sneeze overtakes me, and I start to topple. As I try to catch myself, my hand hits the caps of some of the bottles on the tray, knocking them over. One goes off the edge and *smash!* lands next to the vanity, its sweet liquid spilling onto the dark wood floor.

I freeze.

"Claire?" Mom is standing in the doorway with a question in her eyes.

"Sorry," I say, bending down to pick up the broken glass. "I'll get her a new one. I . . ."

Mom takes my hand and lifts me up into a hug, and I fight the urge to cry into her shoulder.

"What's wrong?" she asks.

But I don't speak. I step out of her hug with a big breath in. I'm getting better at holding in my tears.

"I'll get a broom," I say.

Chapter 15

The day of Brianna's pool party, I pace around my room. Which basically means I walk back and forth from the closet to the window. I notice how ragged the carpet feels under my feet; it's old and the color is fading.

This is the weekend Dad is on vacation, so I didn't see him last night. It's fine. But I think maybe he's gone with a woman, maybe that person who called when we went mini golfing, "K." Who puts an initial into a phone? Someone with a secret.

I stare at Brianna's gift on the bed. I found an old

photo of us together when we were, like, seven, one that was good enough that my mom ordered a hard copy of it at some point. In the moment I found the picture, I thought it would be a perfect present. I made a paper frame for it, and I wrote our names in this bubbly lettering we've been practicing. But when I look at it now it looks like a piece of paper with silly drawings, like something a four-year-old would give at a birthday party, or maybe just like the card part of a gift. I also couldn't figure out how to wrap it, so I slid it into a brown lunch bag with a ribbon at the top and I wrote, "To Brianna, ♥ Claire."

I frown into the mirror above my dresser. The bruising around my eye has faded a lot, and if I wear sunglasses no one will notice, but I wish I had a new bikini. Or at least a cool cover-up. I hate that Brianna and Eden have already seen my new suit. And they know it's not even new-new. Why did I tell them that? I stand on tiptoe in front of my half mirror, trying to make it more full length so I can be sure I look okay.

Forget it, I'll wear my one-piece bathing suit from last

year. I turn around and open my middle drawer, but I don't see the suit, so I start rifling. It's black and white with a geometric pattern. Only Brianna and Ronan have seen it, so maybe Eden and everyone else will think it's new.

Just as I've convinced myself that I *have* to wear that suit, that I can't possibly wear Gemma's bikini, Mom yells, "Ronan's here!"

Ronan. We're driving him to the party, of course.

"Wait a sec!" I snap back, and Mom must hear the edge in my voice because she pops her head into my room.

"What's up?" she asks quietly.

I'm still digging in the drawers, the bottom one now, after I didn't find my suit in the middle one even though I took out all the clothes and tossed them on the floor.

"Nothing!" I say through clenched teeth. "I'm just trying to find my bathing suit."

"Uh . . . you're wearing it." Mom laughs, light and easy, but when she does I feel my face crumble, and I do that silent cry thing. Because the only worse thing than crying is to have Ronan know that I'm crying.

Mom turns and pokes her head out into the hallway. "Hey, five minutes, Ronan, okay? Can you wait on the porch?"

I hear the screen door close behind him, and I let out a tiny little sound. I don't have time to cry!

Mom sits on my bed and pulls me onto her lap like I'm a little kid.

"Hey, hey," she whispers, smoothing back my hair and running her fingers over my face. She doesn't ask more questions, she just lets me breathe in her arms for a minute.

I feel myself calm down, and I wipe away the tears that escaped.

"Claire, if you're nervous about the boy-girl party—"

"I'm fine!" I snap at Mom. *Gah!* She doesn't understand anything. Who cares that boys will be there? Is *that* what she thinks is bothering me? She has no clue.

I stand up and go through the mess I've made on my floor, finding a plain white tee and my cutoffs, knowing

Eden and Brianna will be wearing something cooler, something better, over their suits, which I'm sure will be brand-new, tags off right before the party. I feel myself start to get upset again, so I take a deep breath as I pull the shirt over my head. Then I grab my sunglasses. At least they're new.

"Claire, if you want me to tell Ronan you aren't—"

"I'm going," I say, feeling annoyed with myself for getting upset.

"Well, you look great," says Mom. "Your bikini really suits you."

"Gemma's bikini," I say under my breath.

"What?" asks Mom, but I think she heard me.

I'm out the door as I say, "Never mind."

When Ronan and I ring Brianna's doorbell, Mrs. Foley answers. "Claire! How's your nose?" she asks right away. I raise my sunglasses, and I see her wince ever so slightly. "Ah, still a little yellow, but better!" she says, brightening her voice. Then she turns her attention to my left. "Hello, Ronan."

He says hi with a big smile on his face—we both do, actually. You'd never know we sulked the whole drive over and didn't say a word to each other. Now we're happy sunshine twins. That's what you do when someone opens the door to a party.

But from the second I walk into Brianna's house, I feel like I don't belong at my own best friend's birthday. There's music that seems to be playing from somewhere invisible in the house, all around us. It follows me into the bathroom—I want to make sure there's no evidence at all that I cried earlier—and I look for a speaker but I don't see one.

I tighten my ponytail in the mirror and straighten my shoulders, determined to feel good, or at least not awful, when I walk out to the pool to join the party. The days of being outside have added a rosy glow to my usually kind-of-pale cheeks, and my freckles look less little-girl this summer and more . . . pretty. If this eye would just heal I'd look mostly okay. Deep breath. I pull my sunglasses back down as I exit the bathroom.

I wander out to the patio where strings of lights

are all around the pool, and there are flowers that look like they're from Hawaii—purple and blue, yellow and pink—spread out across a bunch of outdoor tables. Ronan is standing by the sliding-glass doors, so I go to the other side of the pool.

We're right on time, but I don't see Brianna or Eden. There are grown-ups here, though, talking to Brianna's dad. Maybe her parents invited people too. They're all wearing fancy clothes—long sundresses on the women and button-up shirts on the men. I guess adults don't swim at pool parties.

I put my paper-bag gift on a corner bench that's stacked with boxes for Brianna wrapped in red and silver and gold and blue, with curly ribbon decorations. Some even have flowers tied into the gift wrap. I tuck mine in the back so it doesn't show and ruin the pretty display.

Trays of food sit on every open space. There are raw vegetables with different dips, bright platters with strawberries and blueberries and a pretty green fruit shaped like a star, even tiny little hamburgers with tiny little buns and toothpicks with ruffled tops.

This is like a party on TV.

I watch a group of guys from school walk out—Daniel Jacobson and Justin Alonzo, Ryan Crawford and Derrick Malone. They're all on the soccer team together, and I guess they carpooled. Ronan smiles at them and slaps their hands. *Weird.* I rearrange the mini plates on the table near me. I keep my head down. I'm very busy.

When I look up again, Emily Wu and Gwen Forester have arrived, along with Charlene Goodhall and Faye Chastain, more of their friends. I notice that even though the guys are in T-shirts and shorts, the girls are all wearing summer dresses—long and billowing, every single one. I look down at my own white T-shirt and cutoffs and flip-flops, and my uneasy feeling grows.

Then I see the big crowd begin to part.

Eden stands like a tower in the sliding-glass doorway. Her dress, which looks like it's made of white lace, is flowy on top but with a really short skirt, so her long, bare legs are on display. She has on tall white shoes with thick heels. Her hair is pulled back with a scarf being used as a headband, which shows off her cheeks. They're very high or whatever beautiful cheeks are called. She looks amazing.

I can't hear what she's saying, but her mouth moves quickly, and she's not wearing orange or pink lipstick anymore. Today she's bright red.

Eden stands in the middle of this group of people she barely knows and holds their attention completely. I watch their faces—they are so involved that they don't turn away from her for a second.

"My cousin is more popular than I am." Brianna comes up behind me, and I laugh before I can stop myself, embarrassed that I was staring so hard at Eden, taking in her every detail. Brianna laughs too, like she was joking. Was she joking? I can't tell what she really thinks.

Also how did I not notice Brianna coming outside? She looks fancy too, in a heart-patterned dress with a bow at the center. Her hair is smooth and shiny, like someone professional brushed it.

I tug at my T-shirt. "Happy birthday." It's awkward that I'm sort of mad at Brianna but she doesn't know. "You look pretty."

"Thanks," she says, not noticing or at least not mentioning that I'm like six degrees of less-well-dressed than everyone else at this party. "Hey, your nose looks better."

"These help," I say, pointing to my sunglasses.

"Attention, attention!" Brianna's mom is clapping her hands as her dad taps a fork on his fancy tall glass. People get quiet, and everyone turns to Mrs. Foley. "Thank you for coming to Brianna's twelfth birthday party!" A small cheer rises, and I clap a little. Is that what I'm supposed to do? No one's ever given a speech at my birthday.

"You all know that we've wanted an occasion to host an event at our new home, and this is it!" continues Mrs. Foley. "The band is getting set up now, and we'll be giving tours in a little bit, but in the meantime enjoy the food, enjoy the pool, enjoy the drinks . . ." She pauses and winks at some other adults. "We'll do cake in about an hour, so until then . . . have fun!"

There's a band?

Everyone applauds again, and then a flash of blue streaks by my left. When I turn I hear Ronan shout,

"Cannonball!" He jumps into the pool. A big splash makes everyone laugh, and he pops his head up to the cheers of party guests. Since when is he Mr. Spotlight?

Brianna's mom starts to lean down to say something to Ronan, but then Brianna rushes over and stops her, waving her hands. Her mom stands up, nodding. "Okay," I hear her say. "But when the band comes on the pool is off-limits."

My eyes drift to the group of girls around Eden, who's now taking off her cover-up to jump into the pool. I grab a mini plate and focus on the food table near me. There are little circular rice desserts, so I take one. And even though I don't feel like being social, I muscle up a smile and force myself to walk over to where the girls from school are standing.

"Hey, Claire," says Emily Wu. Some other girls say hi too, and I can feel my smile get softer, more real.

"Hi," I say back.

"God, I wish my mom let me wear shorts to the party," says Gwen Forester. "She was all, 'You have to dress up for Brianna!'"

I laugh nervously. I can't tell if Gwen's making fun of me.

But no one else says anything, and then they all start talking about Brianna's house. How amazing the pool area is, how big it looks from the outside, how even coming down the driveway feels like you're going somewhere special.

I take a bite of the little dessert I brought over—*cough!*—it comes right out again, landing on my mini plate.

"Not a sushi fan?" asks Gwen.

Sushi. I've heard of it, but I've never had it. Never even seen it. But that explains why the bite wasn't sweet. I feel my face turning red, and I force another cough. "I'm getting over a cold," I say, handing the mini plate to a guy in a white shirt and black pants who has appeared at my side, hand outstretched.

This party has a staff.

There are a couple of laughs, but then Emily takes the focus off me: "The jukebox though, you guys . . . I think that's the best part." And Charlene Goodhall sighs in wonder.

I look down, still feeling embarrassed. That's when I notice other people's feet. I see pink and blue and red and orange nail polish, pedicures, on every girl here. I didn't know this was a thing we do now. As I'm staring at my own bare nails, I see Brianna's feet join the circle, toes painted in the All That Glitters gold color Eden had.

A screeching sound comes from the pool deck, and we all turn to look. The band is setting up—there are four musicians with real instruments and a singer who just got major feedback from the microphone.

"Sorry, all. What a way to start!" says the singer. "We're the Crescent Moons, and we've got a song for the birthday girl!"

"Ugh, I told my mom a DJ would be better," says Brianna, sounding exasperated. "Not that anyone listens to me." She puts on a fake smile since people are looking at her, and I feel myself getting upset. *How can she complain right now?*

The band starts to play that old song "My Girl," and to the side of the stage, I see Ronan and Eden drying off from the pool. It looks like Eden didn't get all the way wet—her hair is still perfectly headbanded into a bouquet of curls. She pulls on her dress and points to the back lawn. Ronan nods, and I watch them walk over to another feature of Brianna's party that I hadn't seen yet—one of those photo booths that gives you a strip of pictures in five minutes. I thought those were just in bowling alleys and at theme diners, not like an at-home thing you could have. There are a few people waiting for the photo booth, and Ronan and Eden join the line.

Suddenly I feel my sunglasses being ripped off my face, and Daniel Jacobson shouts, "Let's see the shiner!"

I grab at Daniel, but he's holding my sunglasses above his head.

"Ooh, someone got a good punch in!" he says, laughing. I can tell everyone around me is studying my face now too, and I just want my sunglasses back. I feel desperate to get them.

"I hit the pool floor," I say through clenched teeth.

"*Whatever*," says Daniel, laughing and tossing my

glasses toward me. I'm not ready, and they fall to the ground with a clatter. When I pick them up I see a scratch on the lens. My new pair.

"Does it hurt?" asks Gwen, leaning in for a look at my face before I can get the sunglasses back on.

"Not anymore," I say, trying to shrug off what just happened. Daniel's back with the other guys now, and I attempt a smile as I look over at the pool. "I do *not* recommend diving near the shallow end."

The girls laugh softly. This is their third laugh at me, or about me, not that I'm counting. Deep breath. *It's okay.*

"You guys, Ronan Michaels got *hot*," says Gwen. I look up, and her eyes cut to me. "Don't tell him I said that, okay, Claire?"

"I wouldn't," I say. Why would I tell him that and make his head get all big? He's already distracted by Eden, and I don't need him thinking he's the king of seventh grade next year.

"I think my cousin noticed too," says Brianna.

I follow her gaze to Ronan and Eden by the photo booth. Eden is so close to him. They're huddled together, next in line to go behind the curtain. Ronan says something, and Eden throws her head back to laugh.

"You should go get in the photo," I say, grabbing Brianna's arm and pulling her toward Ronan and Eden. "It's *your* birthday!" I'm suddenly desperate to make sure Brianna is in their photo strip too.

"Claire, stop," says Brianna, but she's laughing and she lets me lead her to the line. I push her up to the front next to Eden, stepping back at the same time. "I guess I'm photobombing," she says to her cousin.

Eden puts her arm around Brianna and smiles. "It's an honor, birthday girl," she says. Then they head into the booth. I watch their legs move around below the curtain as they try to fit into the frame, and I see the flash pop once, twice . . . I can't take it. I want in!

I pop my head in right before the fourth and final flash. Ronan yells, "Claire!"

When the strip comes out there are three photos of Brianna, Eden, and Ronan looking cute and silly and serious. And then one of half my face blocking most of the frame while Ronan scowls at me. You can just see the top of Eden's hair and one of Brianna's arms behind me.

Okay, that backfired.

It seems like everyone is annoyed at me, so I grab a plate and some fruit and sit by myself in one of the pool chairs next to the dance floor. Beside me there's a pile of fluffy towels—all the same pattern, yellow-and-white stripes—that match the pillows on the outside furniture. We've had our towels for as long as I can remember. I just stopped using the one with the little hood for a baby last year. I cannot imagine having extra towels that match furniture.

Brianna's dad calls her to the front for a daddy-daughter dance, and I watch them stand together as the music starts. He bends down a little so she can put her arms on his shoulders, and they move slowly together, around in a circle. They look stiff, but it's still a cute picture. People are taking phone videos all around the dance floor. Mr. Foley has a glass of champagne in one hand, and he keeps raising it to other adults who are watching. Brianna is looking around and smiling at everyone. I'm staring at her but she doesn't even see me. I feel like it doesn't even matter that I'm here.

I pop a blueberry into my mouth and attempt to shake off my mood. I hear my mom in my head: *If you're okay with your life, everyone else will be too.* I close my eyes for a second and I try to remember that we may know other people's bathrooms—and even, in the case of Brianna's house, the songs they play in the bathroom—but we don't know their real stories.

What doesn't make sense right now is that I *know* Brianna's story. She's my best friend. Or was. And now she's like this . . . rich girl. The food, the flowers, the photo booth, the *band!* They're all here just because it's her birthday. I can't believe how lucky she is.

The song ends, and Brianna and her dad part. She kisses him on the cheek and then heads in my direction. Maybe she does see me here after all.

She sinks down on the pool chair next to me. "Ugh, when will it be over?" she asks.

"What?"

"All this," she says, waving her hand around like a snob.

I can feel the anger building in my chest now. "God, Brianna," I say. "How spoiled are you?"

"Spoiled?" She looks surprised.

"Yeah," I say. "As in spoiled brat. Look around you! Look at your pool and your house and your . . . your giant birthday cake!"

Brianna's parents are wheeling out a white-frosted cake now—it's taller than either of them and topped with what look like firework candles that give off a blinding amount of light. People begin to sing, and I see Gwen and Emily and Charlene and Faye moving toward the cake, but Brianna is still looking right at me, and I think I see her eyes start to get watery. I feel a twinge of guilt, but I'm too angry to let it stop me.

"Go on," I say. "Your new friends are singing for you."

She stands up slowly and turns away from me. Everyone is looking at her, so even though I don't see it, I know she puts on a big fake smile.

I don't bother to sing; no one needs my voice in this crowd anyway. I watch Brianna blow out the firework candles, letting my eyes go fuzzy as I stare at their sparkling light, and then I just want to go home. I scan the crowd for Ronan.

He's standing with his back to me, talking to Daniel Jacobson, Justin Alonzo, and the other soccer boys. I wanted to avoid Daniel for the rest of the party, but I walk over anyway to ask Ronan to call his mom to come get us. When I get closer, I hear what Daniel's saying. "You know you live in a trailer park when . . ." He pauses, his smile growing. "You wonder why the gas station bathroom is so clean," he finishes.

Everyone laughs, even Ronan, his shoulders going up and down, up and down. Justin slaps Daniel on the back. "Classic, man."

My mouth falls open a little bit, I can't help it, and Ronan turns around and sees me standing behind him. His smile dims a bit as our eyes lock.

I spin on my heels, expecting Ronan to call out, "Claire!" I listen for it, actively listen for it, as I stride through the house and out the front door. Then I march down the long tree-lined driveway, still straining my ears for the sound of someone following.

But I don't turn and look back. And I guess I wouldn't have seen anyone anyway, because I get all the way down Forest Grove Road—to the place where I have to cross a highway to get home—before I stop. I check both ways and race across the road when there's a gap in cars, feeling reckless and angry and alone.

Chapter 16

I high-step through the unmowed field in the middle of Twin Pines Park, and I think about how perfectly tidy Brianna's lawn is. Here, there's a pile of rusted metal tools that a man called Stubby left when he moved, plus a heap of old tires. When we were little, Ronan and I used to set those up in an obstacle course, until the owner came by and told us we couldn't touch anything on the property because it would cost him money if we got hurt. Mom told him he should clean up his tenants' old junk then, but he never did.

When I get to the clearing where I hear the rush of the brook, I exhale and kick off my flip-flops as I shed my shorts and T-shirt. I'm still wearing my bathing suit—I never even got in the pool at Brianna's—and I wade in toward the deeper water, wanting to dunk my head in the small swimming hole. The water is cold and perfect; I go under and come back up. Then I move to the rock where I can dry off and lie in the sun, alone.

The wind makes the bright-green leaves dance above me, and when I turn my head to the side I like the way the sun-warmed rock feels on my cheek. I stay there for a long time, until the light, dimming as evening falls, plays across the water in waves. I think about Brianna's eyes, how they got kind of wet when I called her spoiled. *But she was acting spoiled.* I sigh a loud sigh, annoyed with my own brain for confusing me about how to feel.

I tell myself that I'm not waiting, but I am. I'm waiting for Ronan.

And he doesn't come.

After a while, I jump off the rock and splash through the brook, heading home. As Twin Pines Park comes into view, I see Mr. Brewster's car in his driveway, and then I spot Ronan with Mr. Brewster. They have sodas, and they're sitting in plastic chairs. One is Mr. Brewster's and the other is from my porch.

I'm standing there, unsure of how to walk past them, what to say, when Mr. Brewster sees me and waves. I guess that solves that. I get closer.

"Hello, Claire," says Mr. Brewster, smiling through his shaggy beard.

"Hi, Mr. Brewster."

"Ronan here was just telling me about the party over at the pool," he says.

I raise my eyebrows. "Yup," I say. "It was . . . memorable."

"I've been to a few memorable parties in my day," says Mr. Brewster, leaning on the back two legs of the plastic chair in a way that makes me nervous—they aren't steady. He gazes up at the sky, and I'm standing there all tense, trying not to look at Ronan. Then Mr. Brewster brings the front chair legs down and leans forward, slapping his hands on his knees. "You two should talk!" he says, and it sounds more like a command than a suggestion.

Mmmkay. I'm quiet, Ronan's quiet, and Mr. Brewster

lets his loud words hang in the air for a moment. *Did Ronan tell him what happened?*

He stands up from his chair and Ronan starts to stand too, but Mr. Brewster puts out his hand. "Sit," he says. He pats his chair to indicate that I should sit too. So I do. I sit. And he waves over his shoulder as he walks away from us, toward Mrs. Gonzalez's trailer, I note.

"Anyway," says Ronan, not looking up at me.

"That's not a full sentence, you know," I snap, my anger quickly surfacing again. It's right there, ready to spring on my friends—Brianna, Ronan, whoever's close.

"Come on, Claire, it was just a dumb joke."

I stare at him hard. "You expect me to believe the one I heard was the only one?"

"Jokes, whatever," says Ronan. "They don't mean anything."

"I bet your new best friend Eden thought they were really funny. Was she impressed enough for you?"

"Hey, Eden's nice," he says. "Besides, sometimes it's

easier to hang out with someone who doesn't know . . .
I don't know, everything about me."

"Now I'm hard to be friends with?" I thought the
brook had calmed me down, but I'm feeling madder
than ever.

"That's not what I said." Ronan's voice comes out in
a sigh. "Daniel was kidding around, okay? It was stupid."

"He was making everyone laugh at us," I say. "He
was making *you* laugh at us."

"Claire . . ." His voice is pained, and he pauses. "The
jokes weren't about us."

But that sounds like bullcrap to me. "*You* were
laughing. You made it okay for him to say those things,"
I say. I see Ronan's face tense. "It's wrong to joke that
way, Ronan. It's not *funny*. And it makes it seem like
you think they're better than you. Better than me. And
our families too."

Ronan turns in his chair and faces me. His face is
darker now, serious again, and for a moment I think
he's going to explain himself in some way that I'll

understand and be able to forgive. I'm hoping for that. That's why we're sitting here, right? So he can apologize?

But he doesn't say he's sorry. His voice is bitter as he says very quietly, "They *are* better, Claire. Deal with it."

Chapter 17

Dad comes to get me a little early on Sunday. He rolls up in Charlie and honks, and when I run out to get into the car I glance at Ronan's trailer and find his face in the window—just for a moment.

We haven't talked since yesterday, and I haven't answered Brianna's text either. She only sent one, at least that I got. It said, *How could you say those things to me?* and I don't know how to reply. She was being a brat, but maybe I was harsh. I'm not sure how to feel about anything anymore.

"How's the nose?" Dad asks as we drive. "Mom told

me it was pretty gnarly, but it looks like it's healing up."

Gnarly. Dad uses these funny words from when he was young. "Yeah, it's fine," I say, and I'm glad that Dad didn't see it when the bruising was fresh. He would have freaked out—he gets protective like that.

"How was your trip?" I ask, wanting to change the subject and giving a slight side-eye that I know he can sense.

"It was relaxing," he says.

"Hmm . . ." We're dancing around the fact that Dad may or may not have a woman in his life he likes enough to go on vacation with.

Neither of my parents have had, like, serious relationships since they got divorced. My mom sometimes goes out with friends when I sleep at Dad's, I know that. I'm sure sometimes the "friend" is a guy. But she's never introduced anyone to me, so I know there's no one who's really important.

Dad had a girlfriend when I was little, like, in kindergarten. Her name was Maureen and she smelled like pineapple, but she was only around for one winter.

Since then I haven't met anyone else.

"I'm old enough to hear about things, you know," I say.

"What *things* are we talking about?" asks Dad, all innocent.

"Ladies," I say. "*Loooove.*" I exaggerate the word and make googly eyes at Dad while he's driving.

He lets out a big laugh. "I'm seeing a woman named Karen," he says. "She's nice, she works with horses out on Windsor Farm Road, and that's all you need to know right now."

"Is she the 'K' in your phone?" I ask.

"Yes," he says.

"So you lied to me about her being someone from work."

"No," he says, but his voice is slow, careful. "I didn't lie, Claire . . . I was doing some building for the owner of the horse ranch where she works. So technically, she was someone I saw at work."

"Technically."

"Technically," he repeats, nodding definitively.

"Did she go away with you this weekend?" I ask.

That makes him pause. But he answers after a beat. "Yes."

"Are you going to tell Mom about her?" I ask.

Dad sighs. "I'm guessing you'll take care of that," he says.

"Well, maybe *you* should."

The car gets quiet then.

"Are you going to marry her?" I ask him.

"Now see, that's why I haven't mentioned this to you," says Dad. "I have no idea if I'm going to marry her. I like her and we have fun together and we wanted to go on a trip." We stop at a red light, and he looks over at me. "Cool?"

I nod.

"Okay," he says. "Anything else you want to know?"

"I think I'm good for now." And I am. That's enough. I just wanted him to admit she exists.

We start to drive again. We're headed to Starside Marina, where Dad keeps an old beat-up canoe underneath the dock that his friend Tim owns. We do this at least once a summer, even though I'm not that big on paddling.

When we get there, Dad tells me to take the front end of the canoe. First my flip-flops stick in the mud and then my fingernail bends backward as I shift my weight while placing the canoe into the water.

"Ouch!" I shout.

"Claire, it'll be worth it," says Dad.

He always says that. And I guess it always is. I plan to use my injured fingernail as a reason not to paddle, but I think Dad knows he'll be doing the work regardless. He doesn't even try to hand me a paddle, and I sit in the front, watching the water flow past as my father's arms make the broad strokes that move us out deeper into the lake.

It's hot and sunny, and Dad offers me a dirty ball cap from the bottom of the canoe. I lift an eyebrow.

"Better than a sunburn," he says.

"I put on sunscreen," I tell him, eyeing the mud that's caked onto the Chicago Cubs hat. "And no . . . it's not." Dad gives up and lets the cap drop.

When we get out of sight of the dock, around the bend to an inlet with overhanging trees, Dad sighs.

"Can you think of a more beautiful view?" he asks. I can't, and I say so. "You know, the best thing about nature is that it's free," says Dad, and I think about the brook and how there's nowhere else I'd rather be most days, even this summer when things are all wrong. "All the best things are free, you know," Dad continues.

And then I start to get suspicious. "Did Mom say something to you?"

"Maybe that you've been a little down," he says. It's nice to hear that my parents talked about something other than the schedule—I didn't know they ever did.

"A little." I turn around in my seat to face Dad, but I don't look at him. I kick the bottom of the canoe, and it makes a tinny sound.

"What about?" asks Dad.

I watch one of those big fat dragonflies, the ones who seem like they'd be too heavy to hover in the air gracefully the way they do, land on the edge of the canoe. I reach out my finger slowly to see if it'll climb on, sometimes they will, but it flies away. And then I have nowhere to look, really, except at Dad.

"Things have been weird with my friends," I say, because his eyes are soft.

"Ronan?" asks Dad.

"Yeah."

"Brianna?" asks Dad.

"Yeah," I say. And we're out here on a lake just the two of us and there's nowhere to go and I realize I was set up for this conversation. And maybe I don't mind. "It was weird to see Brianna's big house and her pool and everything," I say. "It made me feel . . . I don't know. She was complaining through her whole fancy birthday party, she takes it all for granted. And when I brought it up with Ronan I thought he would understand, because we're, like, the same. I mean, we're . . ."

"Claire, I know what you mean," says Dad, and I see him smiling. He gets that I'm talking about money, how Brianna has more. He's not going to make me say it.

I smirk. "Right. I know that doesn't matter, but this summer it's felt . . . I don't know, just bad I guess."

"And when you talked to Ronan, what did he say?"

"First he told me I was stupid, and then he said they were better than us."

Dad looks confused. "Brianna's family?"

"I think he meant people with money," I say.

"That doesn't sound like Ronan."

I shake my head. I almost tell Dad about the jokes Ronan was laughing at, but it hurts to even remember that. I can't.

Dad looks out at the water, and I watch him thinking. Then he says, "I'm not sure what's going on with Ronan or Brianna, but what's going on with you is normal," he says. "It's natural to feel a certain way when friends seem to have more than you do. Hell, I'm jealous of Rod's new F150—I wish I could get my hands on a truck like that!"

I nod. "Yeah, I wouldn't mind a window seat and my own bathroom," I say.

Dad smiles. "It's good to dream and imagine what you'd like to have," he says. "There's no shame in it."

"Okay," I say, my mood lifting slightly. "Then I also want a pool and a skylight and a room just for watching movies and pizza and garlic knots whenever I feel like it."

"Dream big, Claire Ladd!" Dad shouts across the water, and I hear it echo. "I bet there are things Brianna wants too, you know. No one has it all."

It's suddenly quiet out on the lake, and Dad turns to me all serious. "Hey, what do you think Ronan wants?"

I look at my dad then, really look at him. He's getting older, even though he's still young for a dad. His mouth crinkles around the edges when he smiles, like he's doing now, and I guess that's from the sun. His eyes look brown, but if you stare at them you'll see a little bit of green in them too. Even some yellow. They're kind, my father's eyes.

"Ronan probably wants a good dad," I hear myself say. And then a tear blurs my vision. I didn't even know it was coming, but as it makes its way down my cheek, another one follows, then another. Soon I'm sniffling and everything and Dad is down on a knee, leaning over in the canoe carefully and patting my back and telling me things are all right.

After a little time, I wipe my face on my sleeve and pull myself together enough to get embarrassed. "I don't know why I'm crying," I say.

"Because you're a good friend," says Dad. He moves back into his own seat, and we bob on the water for a couple of minutes before heading back to the dock.

Chapter 18

When we get back to Twin Pines Park, the sun is in that low place where everything looks golden, like in a dream. I texted Brianna when we got off the water—nothing fancy, just this: *I'm sorry. With my dad tonight. Talk tomorrow?* She wrote back: *K.* And then: *I liked your present.* That made me smile, and now I have my window rolled down to get the breeze. I feel calmer than I have in a while.

But as we pull in, I hear Ronan's voice. Loud and clear and angry.

When we round the turn in front of my trailer, I see Ronan holding his screen door open and screaming into his living room. He's shouting a stream of words we are not allowed to say, and I know he's directing them at his dad.

"—*don't even move off the damn couch! We were fine without you! No, not even that, we were better! Everything was better without you! I wish you never came back at all!*"

I stick my head out the window because . . . I don't know, it seems like someone has to do something. "Ronan! Stop!" I shout. But I might as well be whispering because Ronan doesn't even look my way, and I doubt he can hear anything besides his own anger. Suddenly, Ronan slams the door, turns on his heels, and runs toward the road. He doesn't even seem to see us parked here.

Dad pulls up the brake in Charlie as I start to open the door to go after Ronan. But Dad says, "Stay in the car, Claire." The way he says it means I have to. His voice is like a lock keeping me in my seat.

I turn to look out the back window and see Ronan's figure disappear. He's headed away from the brook. It's getting dark. I don't know where he's going.

Dad gets out of the car and I watch him walk up to

Mr. Michaels, who's standing in the doorway now in his boxer shorts. He's stepping outside, and then my dad is next to him, touching his arm. Steadying him, holding him in place.

I see my dad talking to him; his lips are moving, but I can't hear what he's saying. He's using his quiet voice, the one that means absolute business. After a minute, Mr. Michaels smiles slightly, even pats my dad on the back. Then he goes inside and Dad comes back to the car.

"I should see where Ronan went," I say.

Dad shakes his head. "No. You're coming inside with me till your mom gets home."

"But—"

"Claire, Ronan will be okay," Dad says. "Let him cool off."

I'm about to object again, but something in Dad's eyes makes me go quiet. I'm going inside with him until Mom gets home.

In the trailer, Dad asks what I want to eat. He starts opening up cabinets to see where things are in the kitchen.

"I can make something," I tell him, squeezing past to the refrigerator where I take out the leftover rice mom cooked last night and a few vegetables we have that are gonna go bad soon. I start slicing peppers on the cutting board while Dad sits on a stool next to me. I'm trying to act normal, trying not to wonder where Ronan went.

"Pretty good with that knife," Dad says. He ruffles my hair, and I get the rest of the stuff ready—onions, mushrooms, a clove of garlic that I chop really, really tiny. I put everything in a pan with oil and heat up the rice in the microwave. When the vegetables are done, I put them in bowls over the rice and I get out two eggs.

"This is the secret," I tell Dad.

Then I fry two sunny-side up eggs to put on top of the stir-fry.

Dad and I head to the couch with our bowls.

"Wow!" says Dad when he takes a bite. "Really great, Claire. I'm impressed."

I just chew, trying to swallow down the tiny lump in my throat. We haven't talked about why he's here right now, inside the trailer for the first time since I can remember, sitting on the couch with bowls of rice like this is what we do on Sunday nights.

That's where we are when Mom comes in.

"Rick?" says Mom, and I hear the question in her voice.

"Hi, Bets." She's Elizabeth to everyone but Dad. He says *Bets* with affection, maybe like he used to say it to her, and I feel a little pang.

"I made dinner for Dad," I tell Mom. "There are leftovers. Did you eat?"

Mom doesn't answer me as she puts down her purse and hangs her keys on the hook by the door. She also doesn't take her eyes off Dad.

He reaches for our empty bowls and goes to the kitchen to rinse them in the sink. "Well, I should take off," he says, drying his hands with the checkered dish towel on the counter. "Bets, can I talk to you for a minute?"

My parents go outside to the porch, and I can hear the low hum of their voices but I can't make out what they're saying.

A sweep of headlights sends a beam across the

living room. Ronan's mom is home.

I see Christina getting out of her car and saying hi to my mom and dad. They walk up close to her, and the three of them huddle together as my mom puts her arm around Christina's shoulders.

A minute later, Mom and Dad come back in, and Dad gives me a big hug and a kiss on the cheek that smacks a loud sound. "Next Claireday, I'll cook," he says.

I raise an eyebrow. "Or we could go to the steakhouse."

Dad laughs. "Okay, steakhouse."

Then he smiles at Mom, and she smiles back at him. That makes me feel happy, but I wish it weren't such a bad, weird night.

"Hey, I'm around, Bets," Dad says to Mom. He reaches out and touches her arm lightly. "Just call."

"Thanks, Rick," Mom says. He waves, and she closes the door behind him. Then she flops down next to me on the couch.

"You okay?" she asks.

I shrug. "I still don't know where Ronan went."

"Christina will find him," says Mom. "Apparently he's been taking off a lot this summer."

What? No he hasn't.

I don't think Mom knows what she's talking about. Then her eyes get that weary look in them, and it's like she's talking to the air, not to me anymore. "It's a tough age . . ."

"We are not twelve," I say to her, and she refocuses on me. Then I ask, "What did Dad say?"

"He told me what happened."

"No, I mean to Mr. Michaels," I say. "Did Dad tell you what he said to him?"

Mom looks away, out toward the TV. I guess the TV is easier to look at than a person, even if it's not on. "Your dad told Mr. Michaels that he needs some help."

I swallow, and I feel a chill run through me. "What does that mean?" I ask.

"He's in a bad place," says Mom. "He may need someone to talk to. I think he feels kind of . . . hopeless."

"Can we help him?" I ask.

"That's what your dad and I are going to try to figure out," says Mom. I like the way she said "your dad and I."

I lean into her, realizing that I'm very, very sleepy.

That night when I go to bed, I hear Mom on the phone. She's checking in again with Christina. She sounds calm, and that comforts me as I try to stay awake to ask her when she hangs up, *Did Ronan come home?* But I fall asleep to the soft tones of her voice, sure that he did.

Chapter 19

"He's not awake yet," says Ronan's dad when I knock on their screen the next morning. The front door is open, and Mr. Michaels is on the couch watching TV. He doesn't get up, but he does look over at me when he speaks.

"Really?" I ask. I'm talking through the screen.

He turns back to the TV. "Go get him up if you want."

Normally I wouldn't do that, but I woke up worried.

I step inside and walk around the far end of the coffee table. "'Scuse me," I say as I pass in front of Mr.

Michaels's show. I go down the hallway and notice that there's a cracked hole in one wall.

Ronan's parents' room is on the left, and their door is open, bed unmade. It's Monday morning; Christina probably left for work hours ago.

The closed door at the end of the hall is one I've walked through a thousand times, but today I approach it slowly, like something might jump out and bite me. I knock softly, my voice a whisper. "Ronan?"

No response. A few more knocks.

Still nothing.

I turn the knob.

The bed is made, the room is tidy, like no one even slept there.

"He's gone," I say, first to myself and then more loudly to Mr. Michaels. My voice shakes a little when I raise it, but Ronan's dad doesn't move from the couch or even turn his head toward me as I walk back into the living room.

"He's probably off being mad somewhere," he says.

"We're only eleven," I whisper as I turn to walk out the door. I don't even say bye as I march straight to the brook. Maybe Ronan got up really early and came down here to fish. Some people fish at, like, five a.m.

But there's no one on the bank and when I kick off my flip-flops and wade in until I get to our rock, letting the bottoms of my cutoffs get wet, I know he's not here. I call "Ronan!" one time, but then I stop and make myself stay quiet, because hearing myself call for him like that down here in the woods by the brook reminded me of scary movies that don't end well for the person whose name is being shouted.

He's okay, he's okay. I keep repeating that in my head as I walk back up past our trailers and into Cleland Cemetery to get a good phone signal. Should I tell my mom? Christina?

I remember Ronan talking about why he loves the brook: *No them, just us.*

And before I can think, I text Brianna. She's us.

Claire: Can you meet me at the mall? Need you.

A few beats go by before I see the response bubbles start to move.

Brianna: ofc. 1 hour

I exhale a breath that I didn't know I was holding.

We haven't had a chance to talk about the party yet, about me calling her spoiled. But I needed her help and I didn't think twice about asking. She didn't hesitate. That means a lot.

It's getting to be late morning and there aren't many people at the mall yet. I hear a chime from the register of Razzy's Candy Shop, and I look up to spot Olive Williams's older sister setting out licorice sticks.

Then I see Brianna and Eden heading toward me, and I stand up from my seat at the edge of the lion fountain. Of course Eden came too.

It feels awkward when they get close to me, and I open my mouth to speak but Brianna says, "What's wrong? Is it Ronan?" like she already knew.

I nod. "I think maybe he ran away."

"What?" Brianna's eyes go big. "How? Why? Did his parents call the police?"

"I don't think they know," I say, my words coming out in a rush. "I mean, his dad knows, but . . ."

"Slow down," says Eden, sitting on the edge of the

fountain and calmly patting the space next to her. "Claire, what's the story?"

I sit. It's like she's a grown-up right now, and I'm automatically listening to her. She has her perfect cat-eye liner on again, like the first day I saw her this summer. I tell them about last night, how Ronan and his dad got into a fight. I leave out the specific words he was saying, but they get the picture.

"And this morning his room was really neat," I say. "Like no one had slept there, or even, like, been there in a while."

"Did you tell his parents?" asks Brianna.

"No," I say. "I mean, yes, I told his dad he wasn't home, but he didn't seem to care. Christina was already at work. I don't think she knows." Or maybe she does.

"Could he have just, like, made his bed this morning?" asks Eden. "He doesn't seem like the kind of person who'd up and run away."

"Just because you have a photo booth picture with him doesn't mean that you know him," I say, and she flinches a little bit but she doesn't argue with me again.

I look at Brianna. "His face last night . . . it was so sad."

Brianna bites her lip and looks around the mall, like she might spot Ronan here.

Eden calmly takes out her phone and starts scrolling.

"What are you doing?" I ask her.

"Looking for clues," she says, leaning in toward me.

Of course.

We go right to Ronan's profile and there's the picture from the lake. But it's the latest one.

Eden gets us to the page where all his posts are displayed, and I peer at the tiny images. There's a fish he caught, a pretty shot of Mrs. Gonzalez's tomatoes, and a selfie taken super close-up. But I spot something in the background—a Darth Vader poster.

"I know where he is," I say.

Chapter 20

As I grab the rungs to climb up to Gemma's tree house, my heart is pounding. We took the bus here, Brianna, Eden, and I, and we rode mostly in silence. Everything around us felt heavy. We had to sneak into Gemma's backyard, but I didn't see her dad's car, and I knew how to reach over and unlatch the gate. I asked Brianna and Eden to wait below.

I'm going up alone.

When I get to the top of the ladder, I take a deep breath. *What if he isn't here?*

But then I push open the hatch and poke my head up. There, in the corner of the tree house, is Ronan.

He's asleep in his army-green sleeping bag, curled up in a ball. Next to him is Ellie the lizard in a small portable cage. So I guess he's not alone.

I signal down to Brianna and Eden with a thumbs-up, but also a *shh* finger to my lips. Then I flash a hand at them—*give me five minutes.*

I step inside the tree house and close the hatch quietly. The smell is so familiar, like pine and playdough, and the heavy humidity makes it even stronger. It's going to rain today.

Moving close to Ronan, I sit down, knees to my chest. Asleep he looks like he's five years old, lips parted slightly, hair mussed, eyes closed. I'm staring at his lashes when they start to flutter, and when he wakes up, the blue of his eyes almost makes me gasp.

"Hi," I whisper.

"Hi." His voice is soft too, and he still looks like a kindergartener. He half smiles at me for a split second, but then he realizes where we are. Where I found him.

Ronan sits up quickly. "I was just—" he starts, but I cut him off.

"You don't have to say anything."

He nods, gently kicking off the sleeping bag and leaning back on the wall of Gemma's tree house beside me.

"You okay?" I ask after a minute.

Ronan smiles quickly and shrugs, which I guess means *maybe*. Then another beat goes by in silence, but finally Ronan says, "I used his phone."

Right. For the "lake" picture. "And your dad got mad?"

"No," Ronan says. "I took it. Stole it, really. But he didn't even seem to notice it was gone."

"That's lucky," I say.

But Ronan turns to me and looks in my eyes. "No, it's not," he says. "He doesn't do anything. He doesn't see anything." Ronan pauses, pulling at a thread near the zipper of his sleeping bag, and I stay quiet. "I couldn't take it anymore. Him just sitting there. So I threw the phone at him last night, I said all the things I've been thinking all summer."

I suck in a breath and let it out slowly, remembering

the words I heard Ronan shouting last night.

"I still don't know if he got off the couch," Ronan adds.

"He did," I say. "My dad talked to him. I think maybe my dad is going to try to . . . I don't know, help?"

"Oh," says Ronan.

And when I look over at him, I see that he's about to cry, or is maybe already crying a little, or something. His eyes look wet. I stare at the window so he won't feel . . . I don't know, like he can't cry. He can.

"Hey, Ronan," I say quietly.

"Yeah?"

But I don't know what to say, so I just go with, "It's okay."

I hear him suck up a lot of snot and his arm moves like he's wiping his face.

Then he clears his throat. "Hey, Claire," he says, his voice solid now, stronger.

"Yeah?"

"I really am sorry I was laughing at those jokes at Brianna's. I don't even know why I was. I just—"

"I get it," I say. Because I do. It wasn't about me, it

was about fitting in and being included.

He puts his hand next to mine, letting our pinkies touch. "I shouldn't have done that," he says.

I feel the heavy air around us shift into something more regular, more easy. It's strange, and kind of cool, how you can sense forgiveness, like it's a person who just walked into a room or something.

In the next moment, Brianna and Eden are knocking on the hatch, and Ronan looks at me with a question in his eyes.

"You said just *us*," I tell him. "Brianna is us."

"And Eden?"

"By default, I guess," I say, giving in.

He nods, mouth turned up now, and I call out, "Okay, you guys."

Brianna climbs up first, then Eden, who looks around the tree house and lets out a low whistle. "Sweet pad," she says, smiling, and we all laugh a little. The laughing feels good, like it's breaking up some of the seriousness.

And then they sit down on the floor in front of us. We're in a square formation of four, our knees close to our chests. Ronan, me, Brianna, and Eden.

I'm not sure where we go from here, but after a few silent moments, it's Eden who speaks. "So are your parents fighting a lot?" she asks Ronan. And I freeze because that's definitely a personal question.

But he actually answers. And not with a grunt. "Not my parents," he says. "My mom is sort of . . . forgiving, or something. She doesn't fight with my dad."

"But you do?" Eden prods.

"I guess," says Ronan. "If you can fight with a blob. I don't even know him. He's just . . . there. And it makes me want to be anywhere else."

He's looking down at the pine floor of the tree house, at the knots that look like characters and shapes if you use your little-kid imagination, and I try to think of something to say that'll change the subject or save Ronan from having to talk. But I can't come up with anything. I look over at Brianna, but she's staring to the side, out the little square window where the leaves are jumping and twitching because the rain has started to come down. Everyone is being so serious. And then Eden talks again.

"So you've been staying here," she says.

I look around the tree house and realize that Ronan must have spent more than a few nights here. There's the cardboard box of snacks in the corner that I thought was Gemma's brother's, but now I realize it's Ronan's. His lucky Transformer is in the window, standing watch, and I think I understand why he asked me to look for it that day. Maybe it helped him to have it here. A solar-powered lamp is charging in the sunlight next to the Transformer. I think about the morning I knocked on Ronan's bedroom window. I bet he wasn't even there.

I look at Ronan with wonder. How did he keep this from me? Have I really been so wrapped up in my own stuff that I didn't notice he was basically living somewhere else half the time?

"Not every night," he says, responding to Eden but looking at me.

"So you don't like being at home," says Eden. "I get that. It's nice to have somewhere to go."

I turn away from Ronan and focus on Eden. For the first time this summer, I see more than just a girl who looks cool. I wonder what things are like for her at home, if she wants to find an escape like Ronan has.

A flash of lightning makes us all turn our heads to the window, and a roll of thunder follows it quickly. The sky is getting dark.

I stare at the side of Eden's face as she looks out the window, and after a minute she raises her eyes to the ceiling instead when she says, "My parents fight all the time. Mostly about me. Or money. Or me and money, like how much I cost and what grades I'm getting and whether I'm worth it."

Brianna reaches over to put her hand on her cousin's. "They do not fight about that," she says.

Eden shrugs as she looks down. "Feels like it," she says. "Anyway, maybe it's better that my dad moved out. The house is quieter, I bet."

"He really moved out?" Brianna asks.

Eden nods, and a tear runs down her cheek. But her expression doesn't change, so it's almost like a single drop of rain somehow got in and fell onto her smooth freckled skin. "My mom told me a couple of days ago."

"Why didn't you say something?" asks Brianna, and Ronan and I look at each other and raise our eyebrows like, *Should we be listening to this?*

"It seemed hard to say out loud," says Eden. "Until just this moment." She sniffs once and brushes the tear off her cheek.

"You could have told me, Eden," says Brianna. And I look over at her, with her sincere brown eyes and her hand still holding her cousin's. Brianna is a good friend. I have to remember that, even when I get jealous of stupid stuff.

And then it's like Eden is reading my mind because she says, "You're having this dreamy summer, Brianna. In your new big house with the pool and your happy parents and your amazing window seat."

"What?" Brianna takes her hand away.

I butt in. "It *is* an amazing window seat." But no one pays attention to me. I was trying to lighten us up, but maybe it's okay to be intense.

"I didn't want to mess up your thing," says Eden. "I just wanted to be the cool cousin from Nashville who fits into your perfect picture."

"You don't have to be that," says Brianna. "And it's not perfect."

"Looks pretty perfect to me," I say.

"Well, it's not. Okay, Claire?" Brianna snaps at me, and I open my mouth in surprise. She's never done that before. "God, I'm tired of people being all 'ooh and aah' over the stupid pool! My parents basically threw a party for *their* friends on *my* birthday! All that catered food and the band and her rules about people not swimming during the *pool* party!"

"Whoa," says Eden.

"Yeah," says Brianna. "Whoa. And you guys want the *window seat*! You can have it. I'm so tired of hearing about the stupid new house. Everyone just wants to walk around and drool over couches." She looks at me then, her eyes narrowing slightly. "Or they come over and call me a brat and then leave without saying good-bye on my birthday," she says, and though she sounded mad when she started talking, I hear the shake in her voice as she finishes, and I can tell she's trying not to cry.

"I left because of Daniel," I say. "He was saying—"

"Things that weren't okay," Ronan fills in for me.

I nod, but I don't look away from Brianna. Right now isn't about me.

"I'm sorry," I say to her, looking into her eyes. "I didn't . . ." I start to say I didn't know how you felt, but really I didn't even try to know. I assumed. "I was jealous of the party and the new house and everything. It seems so great."

"Well it's not," says Brianna, sniffling. "No one asked me if I wanted to move. No one ever asks me anything. Not even, like, how I'm doing."

"How are you doing, Brianna?" Ronan asks. And it could sound like he's making fun of her, but he says it in this nice way, like he means it.

She stops talking and sits there for a moment. "I'm . . . feeling like everything's really changed this summer."

We all nod. This is what I've been thinking too. It seems like things aren't as simple as they used to be. I feel a rush of affection for Brianna, and I think about how weird it is that all these things have been going on in my head that don't have that much to do with her. I guess they have more to do with me. We're quiet for a moment, maybe each thinking about our own version of how stuff is changing.

It's Eden who finally speaks.

"Well, I like it here," she says. "Change or not. My friends in Nashville always act so perfect—it's a lot to live up to. But here . . ."

"We are all steaming-hot messes," I say, finishing with a joke. At first no one makes a sound, and I think my attempt at humor fell flat, or worse, made them mad. But then Ronan chuckles and Eden joins him with a smile and Brianna lets out a big "Yup!" followed by a belly laugh.

"*Especially* Daniel Jacobson," Eden says with a groan, and Brianna shouts, "The flicker!" Ronan knows the story and it seems like Eden does too, because we all crack up and we don't stop laughing for a while. It feels good to laugh, like we're being our real selves here in Gemma Skyler's tree house, which maybe is illegal now that I think of it, but it doesn't feel like we'll get caught. Not today.

Eden's feet catch my eye as she stretches her legs out to the side. She's wearing cute rainbow flip-flops that show off her bright-red nail polish, still unchipped. Surface perfection in *Regal Red.* I look up to her face, and Eden meets my eyes, so I give her a real smile. I realize that it's possibly the first real smile I've smiled at her all summer, that I've been constantly looking at her with a whole lot of thoughts in my head. That she's too pretty, too braggy, too flirty . . . but maybe I've been being too . . . judgy?

Eden smiles back at me. It's not a bold smile, not a flashy grin. It's real.

"You can't see the bruise anymore," she says, and I feel her looking at me, studying my face. Then she says, "I'm sorry about . . . that day."

I take a breath and let her apology sit for a moment. Then I say, "Thanks." Her eyes look relieved, maybe even grateful, and I want her to really know that we're cool. So I say, "Hey, can you show me how to do the cat-eye thing?"

She grins and reaches into her tiny cross-body bag. Eden does my eyes and then Brianna's. She offers to do Ronan's but he smiles and waves her off, and he pulls out a deck of cards and it feels like we're far away from the world as we play Crazy Eights. Then Eden teaches us a complicated game called Spades that she learned at sleepaway camp.

I've never been to sleepaway camp, but maybe people like it because it feels like this. There's rain still falling on the roof, but we are warm and cozy inside the tree house. *No them, just us.* Ronan spreads out his sleeping bag so we have a soft place to sit, and by the afternoon we've almost polished off the Triscuits. Ronan lets Ellie out of her cage, and we all take turns holding her and trying to get her to stick her tongue out, but she'll really only do it on cue for Ronan. He feeds her part of a fig bar.

Finally, an alarm on Ronan's phone breaks our afternoon bubble. "Time to go," he says.

When we finally make our way back to the bus stop, the rain has stopped and the fireflies are starting to come out in the dusky purple light. I texted Mom that I'm coming home from the mall, which isn't a lie. I *was* at the mall briefly.

On the bus, Ronan and Eden are talking, so they go into two seats and Brianna and I sit behind them. It's weird, but I don't mind being two by two this way. I'm glad Ronan has Eden in this moment. He has Brianna too. And me. Always me.

Epilogue

In August, Ronan and I have a small joint birthday party in the newly mowed field at Twin Pines Park. Turns out renting a big mower isn't that expensive, so my dad and Mr. Michaels cleaned up the grass yesterday for the occasion. They've been spending more time together, my dad coming over every once in a while for coffee with Mr. Michaels. They even went fishing in the canoe one morning—and they brought Ronan. My dad is younger, but it's almost like he's being a big brother to Ronan's dad. He got Mr. Michaels a couple of days of work on one of his construction jobs, so things are feeling better.

The Skyler family came back last week, and before they did, Eden, Brianna, Ronan, and I went back for a few more rounds of cards and to clean out every trace of Ronan's summer hideout. Then I let my mom know that Ronan might want to sleep over sometimes. She said that was fine as long as he slept on the floor and we left my bedroom door open "now that you're twelve," and I reminded her again that we weren't twelve yet. But actually, today we're at our own birthday party, so I guess I have to stop saying that. It feels like this summer's changes already happened, though, while I was still eleven. So maybe twelve is just a number.

The party invitations for today went to my family and Ronan's, plus our neighbors and Brianna and Eden. When Mrs. Foley drove up to drop off Brianna and Eden, Mom asked her if she wanted to stay, and she handed her a bottle of beer with lime in it. Mrs. Foley hung out all day, and I heard her laughing with Mom and Christina a lot, so I know she had fun.

I talked to Mom and we told Dad it was okay to bring "K," but he said, "Maybe next year," and I think that means he's hopeful about Karen but doesn't want to push it. He's been actually coming to the door when he picks me up, and handing Mom the child support checks himself. I like having him around Twin Pines more, for Mr. Michaels and for myself. I didn't know I wanted that.

Next week Eden goes back to Nashville, and she's nervous about how things have changed there. She doesn't know what to expect with her parents. I know that because she's been talking to us, and getting all of us to talk too. Turns out she's not only a talker but also a listener. I hope she comes back next summer, and I told her so.

Today wasn't perfect. Ronan's dad was pretty quiet and he didn't stay out all day—he took breaks to go back to their trailer, but I think he did his best. He started "talking to someone," I overheard Mom say, which means like a therapist to help him with his depression, and part of that is spending more time outside, I think. He and Ronan turned over all the dirt in their garden plot last weekend, and Mrs. Gonzalez gave them a few cuttings from her plants. I'm hoping they can grow something there.

One of the best moments today was when Brianna and Eden handed me a big box tied with a lavender bow, and I opened it to find the pale-blue dress I'd tried on with Brianna at the mall earlier this summer. I almost started crying right then, and Brianna hugged me and whispered, "My mom insisted."

I ran over and gave Mrs. Foley a big hug. "I cleared it with your mom first," she said, and then I saw Mom watching us from across the grass, smiling, so I ran over and hugged her too.

Dad handed a small envelope to Ronan then, and I peeked over his shoulder to see what it was. Inside were three tickets to a baseball game. Ronan looked at me. "It's for both of us," he said.

But Dad shook his head. "I know my daughter better than that," he said, punching Ronan's shoulder softly. "No, that's for me, you, and your dad." Then he pulled Ronan in for a quick side hug, and even though Ronan put his head down I saw his big smile.

When our cake came out, it had those same firework candles like Brianna's had, and it lit up all of Twin Pines Park. Mr. Michaels came back outside to the porch to sing "Happy Birthday" with everybody, and he stayed out for a while. Mrs. Gonzalez and Mr. Brewster both jumped when they saw the flames and then they moved closer and I swear I saw their shoulders pressed together for a second before they smiled and moved apart. It's funny, I used to think of Mrs. Gonzalez as the older lady next door, but now I can see she's not *that* old. Her garden was always there, poking up every spring, and her wildflower field has been a part of my dreams, but this summer I started to see *her*, Mrs. Gonzalez herself.

Rocky was sniffing around the whole time, but he didn't bark at Ronan's dad at all. Late in the evening, I saw Rocky go over to Mr. Michaels on the porch and show his belly for a scratch.

At the end of the night, after the firework candles were out and everyone was full of cake and lemonade and the quiet Prius drove off into the darkness, Ronan's parents went inside.

"Can I help clean up?" my dad called to Mom loudly, and to my surprise, she said yes. He followed her into the kitchen, carrying chip bowls and a pitcher. And then Ronan and I sat, side by side, on my porch step.

Mr. Brewster and Mrs. Gonzalez were still standing in front of her trailer, talking, and Ronan bumped my shoulder.

"You were totally right about them," he whispered.

I smiled. "I know." Then I reached into my back pocket and handed him a birthday card.

"I hope this is an original Claire Ladd," he said.

"Of course." He put his arm around me, and I started to feel tingly. I got nervous about what was in the card—a picture from when we were five and a promise to always be his friend. "Read it later," I said.

He nodded, his blond hair, *Harvest Gold*, falling in front of his eyes. Then he kissed the side of my head really hard. "Whatever it says, I'll keep it forever," he said.

Then Ronan stood up and walked back to his trailer. When he opened the door I saw his dad standing in the kitchen, helping his mom with dishes. That made me smile.

"Clairebear," called Mom. "Come inside. We've got something for you."

When I walked into the trailer, Mom motioned for me to follow her to my room. There was Dad, arms outstretched, gesturing like a game show spokesmodel.

"What are you . . . ?" I started to giggle as he made jazz hands, but then I saw he was pointing at a bench in front of my window with a pretty blue cushion to sit on. It blended right into the sill, the perfect perch for reading or daydreaming while I look out onto Mrs. Gonzalez's wildflower field.

I lost my breath for a minute and then I whispered, "A window seat."

Mom was practically bouncing up and down with excitement. "Your dad built it. I made the pillow. Do you like it?"

I couldn't answer, but I buried my face into her body as she wrapped me in a big hug. Dad came over too, squeezing my shoulder, and I felt a lump in my throat. Not because of the perfect window seat, or the fun party, or the new dress, or any of that. I couldn't seem to put into words what I felt, but it was bigger than all the things that I know how to talk about.

"Thank you so much," I said. I leaned back to look right into Mom's happy eyes, and then over to Dad, who was grinning like a goof too. "I couldn't love anything more."

Acknowledgments

Thanks to writer pals who made me laugh, who gave me good title ideas, and who may not even be aware that a comment or a kind word helped me through the I-don't-know-how-to-write-a-book phase that seems to *always* hit when I'm working on a draft. Those include, in no particular order, Kristin Mahoney, Lynn Weingarten, Adele Griffin, Micol Ostow, Lisa Greenwald, Sarah Dessen, Robin Wasserman, Michael Northrop, Sarah MacLean, Judy Goldberg, Jenny Han, Sarah Mlynowski, Emma Smith, Siobhan Vivian, Barry Lyga, Morgan Baden, Morgan Matson, Jennifer E. Smith, Bennett Madison, Corey Ann Haydu, and Emily Jenkins.

To Gayle Forman, Adam Gidwitz, and Raquel Jaramillo, who gave me the hope I needed to keep writing even when it felt like the world turned upside down.

To my parents, who have always encouraged adventure and exploration without fear.

To Laura and Frank Adams, whose generosity helps keep my writing life and my regular life in balance.

To Sophia and Shelby Sonny, who allow me to find time and space to work.

To my agent, Doug Stewart, who is quick on the draw and always looking out for me. And to Jen Klonsky, who gets me, which is the best thing this writer can say about an editor. Catherine Wallace, thank you for shepherding this book as well, especially through its finishing stages.

To the publicity and marketing teams at Harper-Collins, especially Stephanie Boyar and Megan Barlog, for their enthusiasm and thoughtful ideas.

To the ace managing editorial, production, and design teams, with Alexandra Rakaczki, Kristen Eckhardt, Erin Wallace, Alison Klapthor, and Michelle Cunningham.

And to Lucy Truman, who gave so many great illustration options for this cover—and with such spot-on details—that I still can't pick a favorite!

And always to Dave, June, and Ida Lou, who are my heart.